A HUNTER'S DESIRES

Tri-Omega Mates 6

Stormy Glenn

MENAGE AMOUR

Siren Publishing, Inc.
www.SirenPublishing.com

A SIREN PUBLISHING BOOK
IMPRINT: Ménage Amour

A HUNTER'S DESIRES
Copyright © 2011 by Stormy Glenn

ISBN-10: 1-61034-501-0
ISBN-13: 978-1-61034-501-9

First Printing: March 2011

Cover design by Jinger Heaston
All cover art and logo copyright © 2011 by Siren Publishing, Inc.

PUBLISHER
Siren Publishing, Inc.
www.SirenPublishing.com

A HUNTER'S DESIRES

Tri-Omega Mates 6

STORMY GLENN
Copyright © 2011

Chapter 1

Nikolai Miroslav shivered as cold air blew into the tavern room. He glared over at the man that walked and let the cold air inside. Niko would never understand how anyone could live in such conditions.

It was colder than a witch's tit in a brass bra. Like he'd know what a witch's tit felt like. Niko chuckled to himself as he took another drink of his hot toddy. Like he'd know what any tit felt like. Just the thought of that particular bit of female anatomy sent another shiver down his spine. Give him a good stiff dick any day.

Niko wouldn't be in this miserable place if he hadn't been sent here by his brother and alpha, Vadim, and his father, alpha of the Miroslav Pack. He blamed them for being so cold. Them and the Eastern European Council, which reluctantly gave him access to the region.

Vourdala Island and the pack lands overseen by his father, Ivan Mirsolav, weren't the tropics, but they seemed like the Bahamas compared to the frozen territory of the wolf pack he was sent to investigate.

It didn't help Niko's mood that he'd been investigating the area for nearly two weeks and he had yet to find a single answer or meet anyone that might be able to tell him anything about the rumor of a pack filled with Tri Omegas.

No one was talking, at least not to him. The patrons in the tavern and surrounding town were nice enough. Niko had even made some friends among several members of the local wolf pack. He just hadn't been able to find any answers. Niko wasn't even sure he knew what the questions were anymore.

Tri Omegas, usually only one born per generation, were appearing at an alarming rate. While it had been good for many of Niko's friends who found their mates, it still concerned everyone.

Anyone *in the know* knew Tri Omegas were special. They had abilities that made each Tri Omega unique, each ability seemingly different. They also needed two mates to keep them grounded and safe, as Niko's best friend, Viktor, discovered when he found his mates, Ryland and Gregory.

Ryland hadn't even known he was a Tri Omega until he was told. Tri Omegas' abilities weren't manifested until they were claimed. It was quickly discovered that Ryland was a healer.

Still, it didn't explain why there were so many Tri Omegas being born during a single generation. Niko no longer believed it was just a fluke as he did in the beginning. There were too many of them. He just didn't know what it all meant.

Hence, his trip to the frozen north.

Niko frowned and pulled his collar up around his neck as the door opened and another group of people walked in, letting more cold air blow into the tavern. He shook his head when he heard laughter. How these people could be so happy-go-lucky when he was freezing his nuts off, he'd never know.

As the cold wind blew across the room, it carried an intriguing scent that caught Niko's interest. He sat up and glanced around the room, trying to pinpoint the unique fragrance. He sniffed at the air.

Niko's gaze settled on a dark-haired man standing across the room, taking his coat off. He should have been angry. This man was obviously one of the men that just let the cold air inside. Instead, Niko could barely remain in his seat while he waited for the man to get settled in.

Gorgeous didn't even begin to describe the tall figure. Niko usually went for men a little smaller than himself. He liked being the big bad wolf that dominated any situation he was in, including sex. For this guy, he might be willing to change his mind, even if for just one night.

Once the man sat down, Niko stood and walked over. He stopped right beside the man's chair and waited to be acknowledged. It wasn't long in coming. Niko smirked when the man suddenly stiffened and turned to look him over. He could feel the intense gaze start at his feet and slowly work its way up his body until it settled on his face.

"Nikolai Miroslav, but you can call me Niko," Niko said as he held out his hand. "I believe you might have some information I'm after."

"Oh?" The man's dark eyebrow shot up.

Niko almost swooned at the heavy accent in the man's voice. Damn, he liked a deep whiskey voice. It made his cock vibrate. The man's thick accent only added to the experience. "Your name and whether you're busy later tonight."

The man looked slightly surprised before he hid it behind a chuckle. He reached out and shook Niko's hand. "Vasiliy Federov, and now I'm free."

Hot damn!

"Care to join me?" Niko nodded toward the door. Propositioning a guy he hadn't spoken more than a few words to didn't faze Niko. He'd done it before, and he'd more than likely do it again. The glint of lust he could see growing in the man's deep blue eyes, however, was another story.

It made Niko ache. It also made walking quite interesting. His cock was trying to bust out of his jeans to get to the gorgeous man walking behind him. Niko could feel the heat from Vasiliy's body and knew he walked close behind him. He couldn't wait to feel that heat pressed up against his, preferably without anything between them.

The moment he stepped out the door and towards the side of the building, Niko yelped as he was yanked around and pushed up against the wall. A hard muscular body pressed up against his, just as Niko desired.

The only difference was that Niko had never been in this position before. He was usually the one pressing someone else into the side of a building. Niko chuckled nervously and tilted his head back to look at Vasiliy. He couldn't quite remember being in this position before either.

"Uh…"

Before Niko could say more, hard lips slammed down over his. Niko tried to inhale, to protest, but there didn't seem to be any air left in his lungs. Vasiliy had sucked it all out with one simple touch of his lips.

Vasiliy took his mouth with a savage intensity. Their tongues brushed together, each of them fighting for dominance. Niko finally groaned and leaned into the man's body, giving up control and letting Vasiliy lead. Niko thought it might have been the hardest thing he'd ever done, but the muscular body pressing him against the wall and the hands mapping out his body made his loss of control almost worth it.

"You have place close by, yes?" Vasiliy asked as he pulled his lips away from Niko's.

Niko nodded and pointed to the upstairs above the tavern. It wasn't much, basically just a room with a bed and a bathroom. It didn't even have a hotplate. Niko ate all his meals around the town. But it was his home away from home at the moment.

Niko started to lead the way, wondering why they didn't go to Vasiliy's place when a slap to his ass drew his attention and made him forget all about where they fucked. He just wanted to get to the fucking part. He didn't care where it happened.

Niko fumbled with the lock as lips moved along his neck. Large, strong hands squeezed his ass sending a shock of arousal spiraling through Niko.

"I can't wait to fuck this sweet ass of yours," Vasiliy whispered against Niko's neck.

Niko froze. He knew they had a bit of a language barrier, but surely the man couldn't have said what Niko thought he did. "What?"

"Open door, majiktoka."

Niko shivered at the strength of Vasiliy's words and concentrated on opening the door to his rented abode. He was quickly pushed into the room. The door slammed closed before he could even turn around to argue with Vasiliy.

Strong arms wrapped around him from behind. Hot breath blew across the side of his face. A body the size of a truck cradled Niko. Large hands started quickly stripping his clothes away.

Niko didn't know what to do. Part of him wanted to spin around and argue with Vasiliy. He wasn't a majiktoka. He wasn't a *little one*, even to someone so much larger than him. Vasiliy might stand several inches taller than Niko, and he might be a good fifty pounds heavier, but that did not mean he got control of the situation.

Another part of Niko just wanted to lean back into the hard body behind him and let the larger man take control and continue to touch him. When Vasiliy's hand wrapped around his naked cock, Niko's thoughts fragmented, and he couldn't think of anything else except the heat filling his body at each little touch.

Niko groaned and tilted his head back as Vasiliy nibbled on his throat. He reached up and sank his hands into the man's dark black hair, pulling him closer. It felt so damn good. Niko wasn't sure he'd ever felt so aroused in his entire life. His skin burned, ached for the feel of Vasiliy's hands.

"I need—"

"I know what you need, majiktoka, you not worry," Vasiliy said. "I give to you."

Niko wondered about that statement until Vasiliy pushed him down onto the bed. By the time Niko rolled over, Vasiliy had his shirt off and was reaching for the buttons of his pants. Niko could only lay there panting heavily. The man was fucking breathtaking.

He started to wrap his hand around his cock as he watched the man drop the last item of clothing on the floor when Vasiliy suddenly reached over and slapped his hand away. Niko's mouth dropped open in astonishment.

"No touching." Vasiliy was gorgeous, but it was clear to Niko the man was out of his ever-loving mind. "Mine to touch, mine to pleasure."

Niko blinked. Okay then, maybe he could put off touching himself for a little longer, but not much. He ached so much he thought he might explode. He yelped, feeling like a ragdoll when Vasiliy suddenly grabbed him and flipped him over onto his stomach.

Niko grunted then started to protest until he felt Vasiliy's very large, very muscular body stretch out over the top of him. "Oh god," Niko moaned.

"Not god, Vasiliy."

Niko chuckled. Vasiliy had a sense of humor. He liked that. He liked it even more when Vasiliy started caressing him. The man's hands were thick with calluses, telling Niko that he worked with his hands for a living.

That was actually kind of hot. Being the beta of a wolf pack meant that Niko dealt with a lot of people that were into politics. It wasn't often he had the chance to sleep with someone that actually broke a sweat for a living.

Besides, the calluses on Vasiliy's hand felt great against his skin. Niko moaned and pushed his body up into Vasiliy's heavily furred one. The man had more chest hair than Niko had ever seen. This must be what people meant when they called someone a *bear*. Normally, Niko was attracted to men with smooth skin, but there was something to be said for being covered by a living blanket.

"So silky," Vasiliy said as his hands moved up and down Niko's body. "Is very nice."

"Glad you like it."

"I do, but this," Vasiliy said as he grabbed Niko's ass cheeks, "this better than nice."

Niko started to protest when Vasiliy scooted down his body. He really liked having the man lying over the top of him. It just felt so damn good. And then he felt his butt cheeks get pulled apart and something wet slid over his tight puckered hole.

Niko shuddered. He'd done a lot of things in his life, some of them pretty kinky. He'd never had someone lick his ass before. And Vasiliy seemed to have a tongue made for licking. It was long and hard and wet.

With each swipe of Vasiliy's tongue against his tender hole, Niko could feel nerve endings in his ass coming to life, begging for more. Every few licks, Vasiliy would rub his thumb across Niko's hole, stretching him little by little.

"Oh fuck me," Niko groaned when Vasiliy's tongue finally penetrated him. Every nerve in his body seemed to be connected to that small little hole, and he was being stimulated from the top of his head to the tip of his toes.

"I will, majiktoka, but you need be ready first."

"I'm ready."

"No, majiktoka, you not. Will take much stretching to make you ready."

Niko's eyes nearly crossed. He wasn't that much in favor of being on the bottom, but if Vasiliy could come through with what he promised, Niko might make an exception.

"You have lube, yes?"

"Nightstand drawer."

"Get."

Niko didn't want to move from where he was, but he was more than willing to get the lube if it meant he was going to get laid all that much faster. He scooted up on his knees and reached over to the nightstand.

He shivered as Vasiliy's hands continued to run over his body. It was hard to concentrate on opening the nightstand drawer and searching around for the lube when his body was going up in flames. There didn't seem to be an inch of skin that Vasiliy didn't touch.

Niko went to lie back down on his stomach when he felt a sharp smack on his ass. "Hey," he said, turning to glare at Vasiliy.

"On hands and knees."

"You could have just said that. You didn't have to hit me."

"Love smack, majiktoka, not a hit. You know if I hit you."

"Hey!" Niko yelped when he felt another smack on his ass, this one harder than the last one.

"You learn the difference in time, majiktoka."

Niko didn't know if that meant Vasiliy planned on spanking him more or hitting him. He started to roll over to ask, not liking the undertones of violence in the man he wanted to fuck, but he was stopped by Vasiliy's hands gripping his hips.

"Look, Vasiliy, you're a very sexy man but—"

"Is good you think so. I, too, think you very sexy."

"Yeah?" Niko was thrilled that Vasiliy thought he was sexy. "That's really—wait, that's not what I meant. You need to stop hitting me. I don't like it."

"You learn to like my hands on you."

"Dude, look, I don't know who you—oh my god!" Niko groaned when he felt two slicked up fingers thrust into his ass. Niko immediately started pushing back and riding them, all thoughts of conversation and protesting leaving his mind in a heartbeat.

He felt incredibly full. Two of Vasiliy's thick fingers were nearly the size of the biggest man Niko had ever been with. He'd heard rumors through his friends that one of them, Jake McAlester, was hung like a horse. He could only dream that Vasiliy was, too.

"You like, yes?"

"Oh yes," Niko moaned. "I like a lot."

"You like this more."

Niko winced when another finger pushed into his ass along with the first two. He knew for a fact that he had never had anything in his ass *that* big. It took a few seconds and a couple of deep breaths before Niko became used to the feeling. Vasiliy didn't move the entire time.

"You are good, majiktoka, yes?"

"Yeah, yeah, I'm okay."

Niko wasn't sure those words were his smartest to say when Vasiliy started moving his fingers, thrusting them in and out of Niko's ass. Niko couldn't keep the small grunts from falling from his lips with each thrust.

"One more, majiktoka, then you ready for me."

"One more?" Niko cried out. He wasn't sure one more finger would fit in his ass. He was pretty damn full right now as it was. He was shocked when a little more lube and a lot more thrusting allowed Vasiliy to push a fourth finger into him.

Niko dropped his head down onto his hands. He felt a bit ridiculous having his head down on the bed and his ass pushed into the air, but his trembling arms wouldn't hold him up anymore.

"Vasiliy."

"You call me Vaska, yes?"

"Vaska."

"Yes, is good."

"Okay." Niko would have agreed to anything. His body was full and caressed and going up in flames. And there seemed to be no end. Vasiliy just continued to give Niko wave after wave of pleasure until it rolled into one big ball that had him senseless.

"Vaska," Niko groaned as he pushed back, impaling himself on the fingers in his ass. "Vaska."

His pulse pounded in his throat. Small beads of sweat trickled down his temples. The air around Niko seemed to grow thicker, making his breathing come out in big rapid gasps. His legs started to tremble.

"Vaska."

"Yes, majiktoka?"

"Please." Niko bit his lip as soon as the word came out of his mouth. He couldn't believe he was begging a total stranger to fuck him. Maybe it was the cold air. It was the only thing he could think of that would explain his lapse in control.

"Tell me, majiktoka, tell what you want."

"Fuck me!"

Niko groaned when the fingers pressing into him suddenly pulled free. He almost cried out with how empty he felt. He gripped the sheets beneath him and pushed himself up onto his arms. Before he could protest the loss of something in his ass, he was suddenly filled again.

"Vaska!" Niko shouted, overcome by how large the man actually was. His inner muscles clamped down on the thick cock pushing slowly into him. Niko just didn't know if they were trying to keep Vaska out or invite him in.

The more of Vaska that filled him, the more Niko's body seemed to accept him. His body clenched. Little spasms of pure pleasure rocked through him, one right after the other. Niko felt like he was burning from the inside out.

"Is good fit, yes?" Vaska asked when he finally came to rest against Niko.

Niko couldn't answer. He was too busy panting as Vaska started pounding into him, the man's massive cock rubbing against Niko's sweet spot with every move. His senses were starting to overload as waves of ecstasy throbbed through him with each forceful thrust.

Vaska's arm wrapped around his abdomen and lifted him up. The man's other hand wrapped around Niko's chest, pulling him back. Niko's legs fell to either side of Vaska so he straddled the man's thighs. His head fell back against Vaska's shoulder.

"Is good, majiktoka," Vaska growled in Niko's ear. "Is very good."

"Yes," Niko hissed. His body cried out for release, and he was so very close. The hands that Vaska stroked over his sensitive skin drove Niko's desire higher, but it wasn't quite enough to send him over the edge. Niko needed just a bit more.

"Vaska, please."

Tickles of pleasure shot through Niko's body when Vaska licked the side of his throat then licked his way down to Niko's shoulder.

"You want, yes?" Vaska asked right before he scraped his teeth over Niko's shoulder.

"Yes!"

Niko shattered into a million glowing stars when he felt sharp canine teeth sink into the soft skin of his shoulder. The pleasure was pure and explosive. The thrust of Vaska's cock, the touch of his hands, and the teeth embedded in his shoulder all sent Niko into deeper ecstasy.

The cock in his ass throbbed, and a fiery sensation filled him just as a loud roar echoed through the room. Niko's head rolled against Vaska's chest as the man made one last powerful thrust and filled Niko with his release.

"My majiktoka!" Vaska shouted.

Niko grunted when Vaska's arms tightened around him almost to the point of bruising. Vaska's heart throbbed against his ear, fast at first then slowing down gradually. He didn't have the energy to protest when Vaska pulled away from him and gently laid him down on the mattress.

Vaska climbed from the bed and disappeared, coming back a moment later with a warm cloth which he used to clean Niko and then himself. Niko's eyes felt heavy as he looked over at the man. He felt lethargic, exhausted. His body had been thoroughly used, every wonderfully aching inch. He just wanted to sleep.

"Vaska," Niko whispered.

Vaska smiled, crawling up onto the bed next to Niko. He pulled Niko into his arms and pressed his head down. Niko rubbed his face in the mass of black hair in Vaska's chest until he found a comfortable spot then closed his eyes.

"Just going to sleep"—Niko yawned—"for a little while."

"Sleep as you wish, majiktoka," Vaska murmured. "I watch over you."

Chapter 2

The dawn was just breaking over the mountains when Vaska decided it was time to rouse Niko. He didn't want to. The man was a pleasure to watch, even when he was sleeping. Vaska had done it all night long. He hadn't been able to take his eyes off Niko.

But the dawn was here, and they needed to go. The longer they remained in town, the more danger their lives were in. Vaska hated the fact that he had put Niko into danger, but there had been no other choice since the moment the man walked up to him at the bar.

"Niko, majiktoka, time to wake."

"Mmm, just a few more minutes," Niko murmured as he tried to roll over.

"Majiktoka, you must awaken."

"Tired," Niko grumbled, trying to bury his face into the pillows.

"We will sleep again. Now we must go."

"Go?" Niko frowned. His eyes fluttered open. "Go where?"

Vaska grinned and stroked the back of his hand down the side of Niko's face. "I am sorry, my majiktoka, but it cannot be helped. I've been in town too long as it is. We must go, for both our sakes."

Vaska leaned back when Niko suddenly sat up.

"Is your English getting better?"

"Is good, yes?" Vaska chuckled.

"Vasiliy!"

"Come, majiktoka, we must pack and go," Vaska said as he rolled to the side of the bed then stood up. He waved his hand around at the belongings Niko had around the room. "You must take only what you need and cannot part with. Leave the rest."

"Wait, wait." Niko rubbed his hands over his eyes then rested them on his knees. "What's going on here, Vaska? You're suddenly speaking perfect English and telling me that I have to pack and go god knows where? What the hell?"

"I will explain everything to you but after we get you packed and get on the road. It's too dangerous to stay here."

"For who?" Niko asked. "I've been here for two weeks, and everyone's been perfectly nice to me. How has that changed?"

"You changed it last night, majiktoka."

"Me?"

Vaska picked Niko's clothes up off the floor and tossed them to the man. "Get dressed, majiktoka. I will explain on the way."

"On the way where?"

"That, too, I will explain on the way. Now hurry, we run out of time."

Vaska quickly got dressed then sat down on the side of the bed to pull his boots on. By the time he was done, Niko was sitting on the other side of the bed pulling his boots on. He was muttering to himself.

"You must hurry, majiktoka. The sun has almost risen."

"Okay, that's enough." Niko jumped to his feet and stormed around the end of the bed to stand in front of Vaska. He crossed his arms over his chest and seemed to set his jaw. "I want to know where we're going, and I want to know now, and I'm not setting foot out of this room until you tell me."

Vaska chuckled and stood. He enjoyed the quick rise of Niko's eyebrows as the man's eyes traveled up his body as he stood to his full height. Niko started to take a step back, but Vaska reached out and grabbed him before he could.

Niko inhaled sharply when Vaska pulled him closer. "You ask too many questions, majiktoka."

"Look, why don't you go and do whatever it is you need to do, and I'll just stay here," Niko said as he patted Vaska's chest. "You can come back when you're done. We'll have dinner."

Vaska chuckled. He wrapped one of his hands around Niko's waist and drew the man closer to his body. The other hand he rested on the back of Niko's neck as he leaned down to kiss the man.

Niko's reaction was immediate. His hands clenched in Vaska's shirt, and he tried to climb up Vaska's body the moment their mouths touched. Vaska chuckled against Niko's lips and moved his hands down under Niko's ass, lifting him up until the man's legs wrapped around his waist. It was an interesting feat considering Niko was only a few inches shorter than Vaska.

Niko's lips were hard and searching, sending the pit of Vaska's stomach into a swirl. Vaska licked at Niko's soft lips with his tongue then pushed inside to explore the recesses of his mouth, giving himself freely to the passion that burned between them.

"More," Niko demanded.

Reluctantly, Vaska knew they could not do *more*, not right now. He pulled away, groaning when Niko chased his lips. "Niko, majiktoka, we cannot. The day is upon us, and we must leave while we still can."

"No, stay."

"I regret that we cannot, majiktoka."

"Why not?" Niko's tone was pleading.

It was all Vaska could do to ignore the way Niko rubbed against him. He groaned and pressed his forehead against Niko's as he tried to calm his breathing and the rapid beating of his heart.

It wasn't as easy as he hoped it would be. Niko was the hottest damn thing Vaska had ever seen, and the man was in his arms, begging to be taken. Any normal man would have given in and tossed Niko on the bed to ravage him.

Luckily for both of them, Vaska was not a normal man. He lowered Niko's legs to the floor then grabbed the man's hands and peeled them off his shirt. Vaska pressed Niko's hands together and held them as reason started to return to Niko's green eyes.

The man suddenly looked startled as if he just realized he had practically attacked Vaska and begged to be fucked again. When Niko yanked on his hands, Vaska let them go then watched Niko back away from him.

"Majiktoka?"

"I don't understand any of this, Vasiliy."

"What is to understand?"

Niko gestured between them with his hand. "This thing between you and me, it's not natural."

"I would disagree, majiktoka. I think it is very natural."

"No, I don't attack a guy at the drop of a hat."

"I would hope not, majiktoka. I would be very unhappy if you behaved in such a manner with anyone except me."

"Vasiliy!"

"Yes, majiktoka?"

"Grrr," Niko growled as he began stomping around. "I have never met anyone so exasperating in my entire life."

"It is part of my intriguing personality."

Niko snorted.

Vaska grinned. He actually found Niko's reaction quite amusing. He crossed his arms over his chest and watched. Niko started mumbling to himself again as he stalked around the room and began shoving items into a black backpack.

Vaska was impressed with how quickly Niko packed and the small amount of items he took. The man traveled light. That was a good thing. They were going to be traveling quickly. Too much stuff would just slow them down.

Niko finally dropped the backpack on the floor in front of Vaska. His eyes narrowed as he waved at the bag then folded them over his chest. "There. Happy?"

"Extremely."

"Enough to explain to me what in the hell is going on?"

"As we travel, majiktoka."

"Okay, there is something you're not getting here. Until you explain to me what in the hell is going on, I'm not setting foot out of this room."

Vaska cocked an eyebrow. Was Niko challenging him? It seemed he needed to show his sexy majiktoka who was top dog, well, top wolf anyway. Vaska struck while Niko's attention was on the bag at their feet. He grabbed Niko around the hips and lifted him into the air. In one fluid motion, he turned and tossed Niko onto the bed, coming down over the top of him.

Vaska had Niko pinned to the bed, his arms held down over his head, and he straddled Niko's body before the man could even protest. Vaska leaned down close until his chest brushed against Niko's.

"You were saying, majiktoka?"

"You..." Niko gasped. "You can't do this."

Vaska grinned, almost as much from the protests falling from Niko's lips as the cock he felt hardening in the man's jeans. "I can't do what, majiktoka?"

Vaska stroked his tongue across Niko's lips, stealing any protests the man might make. He could feel the tendons in Niko's wrists stiffen and stretch as he clenched his hands into fists. He knew Niko was trying to hold onto his control and remain clear headed.

As much as Vaska appreciated Niko's self discipline, it was something that could be very detrimental to getting Niko out of town as fast as he could. He needed Niko to be obedient, not defiant.

"Do you not want to go with me, majiktoka?" Vaska whispered against Niko's lips. He knew he was being underhanded, even somewhat of a bastard. He'd learned that Niko had no resistance to his kisses, and Vaska planned to use that to his advantage. "Do you not want to feel me fuck you again?"

"I…uh…" Niko panted heavily, his eyes starting to go wild as he pushed his body up into Vaska's, the white bleeding out as they widened. His hips started humping into the apex of Vaska's groin. "Yes."

Vaska rewarded Niko's answer by pressing their lips together and claiming the man's mouth with a hunger that belied the urgency he felt about their leaving. Niko's deep groan rumbled through his chest, which vibrated against Vaska.

Niko's rugged vitality captivated Vaska and sent his desire for the man spiraling. He could feel Niko's heart thundering rapidly against him. A brief shiver rippled through Vaska when he felt Niko's tongue brush against his.

"Vaska," Niko murmured.

"My majiktoka," Vaska whispered back as he peppered the strong line of Niko's jaw with kisses, "the things I want to do to you."

"Okay."

Vaska grinned against Niko's skin at his easy acceptance then moved down to the bite mark healing on Niko's shoulder. He stared at the reddened teeth marks, his heartbeat skyrocketing at the site of his claim on Niko.

When Vaska stroked his tongue across the bite mark, Niko cried out and arched into him. Vaska knew this spot was supposed to be an erogenous zone for the man. It was a long held myth in the wolf world. He just hadn't expected it to affect the man quite so much.

Niko's hands were clenching then unclenching. His thigh muscles had gone rigid, but not as rigid as the cock trapped behind Niko's zipper. Vaska could feel it pressing up against him, straining against the denim fabric of Niko's jeans. He ached just as much, the need to claim Niko again almost overwhelming, almost.

Vaska grabbed both of Niko's hands in one of his. He reached between their bodies with his other hand and fumbled with the zipper and buttons on Niko's jeans until he could pull them open and grab Niko's cock.

"I fix, yes?" Vaska started quickly stroking the length of Niko's cock, his fingers tight around the thick erection.

"Oh god, yes!"

"Not god, Vaska."

"Yes, Vaska!"

"Good, majiktoka, very good."

Once again, Vaska found himself rewarding Niko's answer. He tightened his fingers then leaned down again and stroked his tongue across the bite mark he'd left in the man's shoulder the night before.

The myth of the bite mark was solved when Niko instantly cried out and covered Vaska's hand with hot seed. Vaska growled then sank his teeth into the bite mark once more. The sweet taste of Niko's blood flooded across his tongue.

Vaska felt it coursing though his veins like an awakening river. His own cock throbbed in his pants, wanting the same release he had just given Niko. Vaska knew their time was growing shorter with every passing second. Despite the burning need he felt, he couldn't endanger Niko to feed his lust.

Vaska licked the wound clean then leaned back to look down into Niko's dazed green eyes. He released the cock in his hand and brought his hand up, holding it in front of his face. With Niko's eyes pinned on him, Vaska stuck his fingers into his mouth and licked the man's release from them.

Niko's eyes widened even more. The heavy pants that had been slowing started speeding up again. A soft flush of arousal filled Niko's prominent cheekbones. Niko's mouth dropped open, and he licked his lips as if they had suddenly become dry.

Once his hand was clean, Vaska grabbed Niko's face and gently held it. "Next time you take my cock, yes?"

"I..." Niko gasped. "You..."

"I and you, yes."

"Vaska."

Vaska reached down between them again and stuck his hands inside of Niko's jeans. He bypassed the man's softening cock and pushed down further until his fingers grazed across the tight hole that quivered at his touch.

Vaska pushed the tip of one finger into Niko's ass, just past the first ring of muscles. Niko inhaled sharply. His body rippled around Vaska's finger.

"You ache to be filled, majiktoka." Vaska wiggled his finger until Niko inhaled and pushed back against the intrusion. "This hole wants my cock. It begs for me, yes?"

"Yesss," Niko hissed.

"Tonight, I take you again." Vaska licked at the bite mark on Niko's shoulder again as he wiggled his finger some more. He started pushing it in further and further. "I fill this hole, majiktoka, yes?"

"Oh…oh, yes, Vaska, please," Niko groaned.

Vaska lifted his head when he felt Niko yanking on the wrists he held captured over the top of the man's head. "This night, I fuck you until ache is no more, Niko. I make you come many, many times, yes?"

"Vaska!"

"Sadly, is not night, majiktoka, is dawn. Time to leave for us."

"No!" Niko cried out.

Vaska was surprised by Niko's strength when the man ripped his hands away from his grasp and reached for him. He knew Niko was strong. Vaska just hadn't expected him to be that strong. How arousing.

"But first, majiktoka." Vaska scooted down Niko's body until the man's cock was right in front of him. It still stood at full mast, thick and throbbing with need. "We must clean you."

Niko's entire body stiffened when Vaska started licking away the cum covering his cock. He paid special attention to the small slit in the top of Niko's cock, pressing the tip of his tongue into the small slot.

Sweet ambrosia exploded in little drops across Vaska's tongue. It tasted just as addicting as the man's blood. Vaska moved his mouth down and licked the cum away from Niko's ball sac then up each side of his thickly veined cock.

A glance up showed that Niko was mindless with pleasure. His head thrashed back and forth on the pillow. His mouth hung open, soft gasps falling from his lips. Niko's hands gripped the blanket on either side of his body so tightly that his knuckles were white.

Vaska pushed a second finger into Niko's ass. At the same moment, he sucked the man's cock deep into his mouth. He never felt so powerful as he did when Niko shouted and filled his mouth with a second release.

Vaska swallowed and licked until not a trace of cum remained on Niko's body. When he finally pulled his fingers away and climbed up Niko's body, the man didn't even have his eyes open. His chest still rose and fell rapidly as he panted.

Vaska cupped the side of Niko's face until he opened his eyes. Bright shining-green orbs stared up at him. Vaska could see the confusion in Niko's eyes, the sense of wonder. He understood that Niko was shaken by what happened between them and the strange power Vaska seemed to have over him. Vaska gloried in it.

"And now, you are clean, majiktoka."

"Vaska," Niko whispered hoarsely. His hand fluttered against Vaska's chest, and his brow drew together in a confused frown. "How do you keep doing this to me?"

"Do you not like it, majiktoka?"

"It's…I've never…" Niko licked his lips and glanced away.

Gathering Niko into his arms, Vaska held him snugly against his chest. Niko's broad shoulders were heaving as he breathed. His hands gripped the fabric of Vaska's shirt. Vaska didn't miss the rugged, musky smell of Niko as he pressed closer. It called to him on every fiber of his being and told him that Niko was right where he needed to be, confused or not.

"All is as it should be, my majiktoka," Vaska whispered against the top of Niko's head.

"No, it isn't," Niko cried out, suddenly pushing at Vaska's chest. Vaska let him lean back just enough for them to look into each other's eyes. "I don't do this. All you have to do is touch me, and I'm ready to do whatever you want. This isn't me. It's like I have no will of my own."

"Sshhh, majiktoka." Vaska stroked the side of Niko's face again. "It is natural for your body to accept mine, to need mine. That is the way of things, yes?"

"No!"

Vaska chuckled. Niko protested so strongly, yet Vaska could feel the man's body pressing into his as if Niko couldn't stand for them to be separated. "You crave my touch, do you not?"

Niko's flushed face was all the answer Vaska needed.

"Ah, majiktoka, you do crave my touch. You need it like you need air to breathe. There is no need to pretend otherwise."

"Vaska, you're not listening to me, and I know you speak English well enough to understand me." Niko waved his hand frantically between them. "This *thing* going on between us, whatever it is, it's not natural. I don't behave like this. I have never been led around by my dick in my life."

"And yet, you are."

"Vaska!"

Vaska chuckled. "Why do you fight so much, majiktoka? Did you not enjoy yourself?"

"That's not the point."

"I believe that is very much *the point*, Niko."

Niko huffed and dropped his head back against the pillow. "Can I get up now?"

"Of course, majiktoka." Vaska rolled to the side of the bed and stood. He turned back and held his hand out to Niko, taking just a moment to drink in the provocative sight of Niko lying on the bed looking totally debauched.

"Vaska, you have got to stop looking at me like that."

Vaska grinned as he helped Niko to his feet. He was loath to see the man tuck away his beautiful cock and close up his jeans, but time was of the essence. They needed to leave while they still could, no matter how much Vaska wished they could stay and fuck away the day.

"I fear I am unable to stop looking at you, majiktoka. You are beautiful to behold."

Niko planted his hands on his hips and glared. "Would you stop?"

"Stop?"

Niko stomped his foot. "You can't keep looking at me like that."

"I like looking at you, majiktoka. It brings me much pleasure."

"Vaska!"

Niko was indeed a treat. Even with his face flushed red with anger, Vaska thought him to be the most handsome man he had ever seen. He stepped forward and grabbed Niko, pulling him into his arms again. Niko huffed but didn't fight Vaska's hold.

"You are the most beautiful of treasures, majiktoka." Vaska rubbed his cheek over Niko's. "I am a very lucky man."

Niko started to melt against Vaska again. "Vaska, I can't think when you do that."

"You think too much."

"You would say that." Niko snickered.

"I would. We do much better when you stop thinking and just let me pleasure you."

"Vaska!"

"I speak truth, majiktoka." Vaska quickly kissed Niko on the lips then pulled away before the man could protest. "I prove to you tonight when I fuck you again. Now we go. Our time here is passing fast."

Niko just seemed to kind of blink as if stunned. Vaska chuckled and stepped over to grab the man's backpack off the floor before handing it to Niko. "Come, majiktoka, we go now."

"Go where?" Niko asked as he followed Vaska toward the door.

"You see, majiktoka. You like, promise."

"I still don't understand why I can't stay here. This is my room after all."

"Is too dangerous, majiktoka."

"For who?"

"You."

"Me?" Niko skidded to a stop. "Why would I be in danger?"

"You are my mate, are you not?"

"No!" Niko frowned, the backpack dropping from his hands to plop on the floor. "Am I?"

Chapter 3

Niko's mind reeled as he followed Vaska through the quiet streets of town. People were just starting to wake up. The fishermen and those coming home from night shift work seemed to be the only people on the streets besides the two of them.

He still didn't understand why he was following Vaska through the streets instead of sleeping peacefully, snug in his bed. Granted, Vaska was one of the hottest men Niko had ever seen, and he fucked like a dream, but was that reason enough?

Niko was still stunned by Vaska'a declaration that they were mates, and he wasn't sure he believed it. He'd know if he met his mate, wouldn't he? Niko tried to remember everything he knew about being mated.

There was supposed to be some undeniable connection between mates. The need to protect a mate was ingrained in a wolf. It became almost an obsession. So did the need to be with a mate. Being separated was painful, physically painful. More than one wolf had been driven mad after being separated from their mate.

The constant obsessive need to touch between mates was strong. It could be something as simple as a touch or the scent of a mate. It often couldn't be controlled unless they were intimate as often as possible.

Niko suddenly stopped, his mouth dropping open in astonishment. Something akin to fear and elation warred inside of him, making it hard to breathe. Niko rested his hands on his knees and bent over as his head began to spin.

"Niko?"

Niko waved a hand at Vaska. He was beyond speech at the moment, too filled with shock. He felt Vaska's arms encircle his waist, and he leaned into the larger man. Niko realized even as he did it that he was helpless to prevent it. He naturally sought out Vaska as a source of comfort and protection.

He wanted to scream and rant at the injustice of it all. Niko didn't plan on finding his mate until he was old and needed someone to take care of him. He didn't want to be tied down to one person. He wanted to be able to play the field.

The constant worry? Never having a thought to himself? Only being able to have sex with one person for the rest of his life? None of that sounded good to Niko. It sounded like responsibility and commitment, and it made Niko's stomach roll.

"Niko?" A hand brushed the side of Niko's face. "What troubles you, majiktoka?"

"I can't do this."

"Do what, majiktoka?"

Niko looked up at Vaska and almost wept. The man was simply perfection from the top of his black-haired head to the bottom of his boot-clad feet and every inch in between. Niko had just wanted to fool around with the man. He didn't want to be mated to him. There had to be some way out of this.

"I can't be mated."

Vaska's slow, easy grin almost made Niko change his mind. The man really was breathtaking.

"There is choice?"

"There has to be. I can't be mated."

Niko felt a cold chill sweep through his body when Vaska dropped his arms and stepped back. The chill started to freeze inside of him when Vaska crossed his arms over his chest. The thinned-lip expression on Vaska's face didn't bode well for Niko, and he knew it.

"If that is your choice, Nikolai." Vaska's deep blue eyes were hard, flat, passionless.

"It's nothing personal, Vaska. I'm sure you're a great guy," Niko said quickly. "I'm just not ready to be mated."

"As you wish." Vaska's hands dropped to his sides. Niko could see them clench into fists. Vaska's face looked stern and rigid as he nodded. "Be well, Nikolai Miroslav."

"Oh, but…" Niko whispered as Vaska spun on his heels and walked away. Before Niko could stop the man, he was swallowed up in the morning fog. Niko glanced around, feeling weird to be standing in the middle of the streets by himself.

He wrapped his hands around his arms and started back toward the room he was renting. Each step felt heavy. Niko wondered if he'd ever see Vaska again, and then he wondered why such a thought pained him.

Niko liked the guy. He could at least admit that to himself. He liked Vaska a lot. He just didn't think he liked the guy enough to commit for a lifetime. Did he? Niko groaned and walked over to lean against the nearest building. He felt like his head was spinning.

Niko took several long, deep breathes then pushed himself away from the wall. He needed to get back to his cramped little room and get some sleep. He'd gone to bed late last night and gotten up earlier than should be allowed by law. He needed rest. He'd decide what to do about Vaska in the morning…er…after several hours of sleep.

The raucous sounds of laughter and the heavy fall of feet walking on wet pavement suddenly filled the frigid and foggy air. Niko stiffened and tried to see into the dense fog. Not being able to see who laughed so menacingly creeped him out.

The fog was thick and grayish in the dawning light. Niko could only see about ten feet in front of him. But he could hear someone walking around. The sounds seemed to pace back and forth in front of him, never coming too close, never going too far.

"Who's there?"

A low, rumbled laughter filled the air again. Niko lifted his nose into the air and drew in a deep breath. The air was cold and smelled of the sea. The hint of salt and fish was almost overpowering, but not enough that Niko missed something else.

The scent was faint, but it was there. It held the taint of danger. Just enough to give Niko pause but not enough to make him feel overly threatened. Still, Niko didn't like facing an unknown foe.

"Who's there?" he asked again.

When he received no answer, not even the threatening laughter from a moment ago, Niko decided this was one place he didn't want to be. He secured his backpack on his shoulder and hurried down the street, trying to keep his eyes and ears open for any possible attack.

The hairs on the back of Niko's neck stood on end, and he knew he was being followed. He could even hear the soft footfalls of someone trying to hide the fact that they were following. Niko had spent too many years getting in and out of trouble with his brother, Vadim, and their friend, Viktor, to not be able to pick out the sounds of someone tracking him.

Niko moved faster but tried not to look like he was. He didn't know who was following him, but he wanted to lose whoever it was, and before he reached his rented room. Pretty much everyone in town who knew Niko knew where he was staying. It wasn't a big secret. Still, he would feel better when he was inside and just a bit more protected.

"Fuck!" Niko shouted when a sudden sharp pain seared through his arm. He looked down and was totally shocked to see blood dripping through the rip in his shirt. There was a perfectly straight cut on his arm about an inch long.

Grating laughter filled the air, and a shadow passed Niko so fast he only saw a blur of movement. Niko gasped as he felt another pain in his other arm. He looked down to see a similar bleeding cut.

"Who are you?" Niko called out as he looked around frantically. "Why are you doing this?"

"You will die, abomination."

Niko stilled his body, but he couldn't stop the sudden thundering of his heart. There were a lot of reasons that someone might think he was an abomination, everything from being a wolf to being gay.

Niko felt another cut then another as the shadow circled him, staying just far enough out of range that Niko couldn't make out who was attacking him. He could only see a shadowy shape moving quickly around him so fast that Niko had a hard time tracking him.

"Who are you?" Niko shouted again.

Niko grunted as he was suddenly caught and spun around then shoved into the building next to him. His body was blanketed by a large form from behind, holding him against the cold bricks of the building. Hot breath beat down on the back of Niko's neck.

"I'm the one that is going to kill you, abomination," a voice growled into Niko's ear.

"I am not an abomination."

"You kill for pleasure," the voice growled. "You spread your disease to everyone you touch. You take and you kill and you need to die."

Okay, so whoever this was wanted to kill Niko because they knew he was a wolf and not because he was gay. That at least meant Niko didn't have to hide what he was. He could use all of his wolf abilities to protect himself.

"I've never killed anyone that didn't deserve it."

"You lie!" the man snarled, and Niko now knew it was a man. He'd never met a woman strong enough to hold him, not even one that could shift. "But I would expect no different from one of your kind. You're all lying dogs."

"My kind?" Niko snapped. "There's nothing wrong with *my kind*."

"You're a killer."

Well, Niko didn't think he could argue with that. He had killed but only when he needed to, when his life or one of his pack was threatened. He never killed for the fun of it, although he had heard of wolves that went rogue and killed for pleasure. They were usually hunted down by the council enforcers and eliminated.

"You're going to find out exactly what kind of killer I am if you don't let me go."

The breathing on Niko's neck became stronger, heavier. Niko could just see the outline of a man's face out of the corner of his eye.

"I'm not scared of you, abomination."

"The name is Nikolai, not abomination."

"Do you think I give a fuck what your name is?" the man growled. "You're still going to die."

Niko grunted when he was suddenly slammed against the side of the building again. He could feel pain starting to radiate out through the cuts on his arms and the new scrapes on his face from the brick. Niko allowed his razor-sharp claws to extend out of his fingertips and his canine teeth to drop down in his mouth. He was really starting to get tired of being treated like a ragdoll.

Niko reached down with his hand and drove his claws into the man's leg. He heard the man grunt, but no other sound came out of his mouth. He knew the man had to be in pain. Niko's claws were embedded in his thigh.

Niko used the man's momentary astonishment to jerk around in his arms. He had just a moment to take in a shock of sunlight-blond hair and milky blue eyes before the man started struggling against him.

"My name is not abomination!" Niko snapped as he started slashing at the man with his free hand. He could see bloody streaks across the man's chest and knew he'd hit his target but so had the man. Niko felt shards of pain blast across his chest and arms as the man stabbed at him with a knife.

Niko knew he had a good chance of coming out of this fight alive, but only if he could subdue the man enough to get away from him. He might be a wolf, but he could die just like anyone else. It just took a little longer.

When the tall man leaned closer to him, Niko saw his chance and sank his teeth into the skin right over the man's thick pectoral muscles. Shock at the sweet taste of blood flooding his mouth allowed the man to jerk away from Niko.

Niko grunted in pain as he was shoved hard and hit the brick wall. His head slammed back with a painful thud. He was thankful for that brief bit of pain a moment later when the man's knife narrowly missed his throat. It would have been a killing blow.

"I will kill you, abomination."

"Nikolai," Niko choked as his vision began to dim, his head spinning with pain. Niko suddenly didn't know if he was going to get out of this mess alive and regretted talking to Vaska the way he did. But maybe this was better. Vaska wouldn't have to have an asshole for a mate. "My name is Nikolai."

* * * *

Niko went from a world of blackness and nothing to awake and filled with pain in an instant. He inhaled sharply, his fingers curling into the blankets covering him. He kept his eyes closed and used his other senses to figure out where he was.

Most of the scents floating through the air were different than he had ever smelled. There was a strong smell of fresh country air for one. Niko could also smell eucalyptus in the air along with the faint scent of apples.

There was obviously a window or something open, because Niko could feel the warmth of sunshine on his face and a slight breeze blowing across his face. He could also hear birds chirping in the distance as well as the sounds of muffled voices and footsteps. But they came from far away, so Niko wasn't that worried about them.

He was more concerned with the slight breathing he could hear inside the room. Niko opened his eyes just a bit, just enough to see a small figure standing next to him. His vision was blurry, so it took a moment for the form to take shape.

When it did, Niko frowned and opened his eyes even more. He didn't understand where he was or why there was a little girl with chestnut curls standing next to him. She had her thumb in her mouth and a blanket held tightly in one arm. They stared at each other for the longest time.

"Hello," Niko said softly.

The little girl suddenly went running from the room, screaming at the top of her lungs. Niko groaned. He closed his eyes and grabbed his head, pain thundering from one side of his skull to the other. This would be why he didn't like kids.

Niko felt like his head was going to explode. The ringing was the worst. It made his head spin and his stomach threaten to rebel. Niko took several slow and deep breathes. His stomach started to settle, and his head stopped spinning.

When he felt like he might be able to handle it, Niko opened his eyes again. He quickly glanced to the side of the bed to make sure the little demon hadn't come back then breathed a sigh of relief when he found the spot empty.

"Oh thank god," Niko whispered as he closed his eyes again and settled his head back on the pillow.

"I told you before, Nikolai, it's Vaska, not god."

Niko's eyes snapped open, and he looked down toward the bottom of the bed. Whatever air he had in his lungs wasn't sufficient to feed his shocked gasp of surprise when he saw Vaska standing at the end of the bed, his arms crossed over his chest. Niko started coughing violently.

Vaska raced over to the side of the bed and sat down. He helped Niko sit up and thumped him on the back. Niko waved him away, pretty sure the man didn't understand that the thumping was only making it worse. Vaska was a very strong man, and Niko felt like his back was being beaten.

By the time he finally stopped coughing, Vaska held a cup of water in front of him. Niko took several grateful gulps of the sweet-tasting water, groaning in protest when Vaska pulled the cup away. Niko eyed Vaska cautiously as he slumped back against the bed and pillow.

"Vaska."

"Nikolai," Vaska replied simply as he set the cup back on the nightstand then turned back to face Niko.

"Where am I?"

"You do not remember?"

Niko didn't miss the way Vaska's dark eyebrow raised up in surprise. It was very cute. "I remember having my ass handed to me."

Vaska smirked. "Yes, that would seem to be what happened."

Niko cocked his head to one side. "It's amazing to me how perfect your English becomes when you want it to be."

"Is good, yes?"

Niko rolled his eyes. "Vaska!"

Vaska chuckled and patted Niko's hand lightly. "There are things you have yet to understand, Nikolai."

"So explain them to me."

"In time, Nikolai."

Niko wanted to growl with frustration. "That seems to be your answer any time you don't want to answer my questions. Why is that?"

"And I'm afraid, for now, it will continue to be my answer."

"Why?" Niko wasn't sure he liked the way the smile fell off of Vaska's lips and they pressed together in a grim frown. A shiver of alarm shot through him. "What aren't you telling me, Vaska?"

"I did tell you, Nikolai. I warned you that we were in danger. Not being mated seemed to be more important to you at the time."

Niko sighed deeply. He could hear the pain in Vaska's voice and knew he had hurt the man with his denial of their mated status. He was sorry for that, but he just couldn't wrap his head around the fact that he was mated. It wasn't something he planned in his life, not for a very long time.

"Look, Vaska, I'm sorry about that. It really has nothing to do with you. It's not personal."

"My mate refuses to accept me. I'd say that was very personal."

"You don't understand."

Vaska jumped to his feet and started pacing beside the bed. Niko watched him until he stopped suddenly. Vaska pushed his hand through his dark hair then looked back at Niko.

"So, explain it to me then."

"I'm not sure I can." And Niko wasn't sure he wanted to. He had his reasons for not wanting to be mated, but as he tried to put them into some semblance of order so he could explain them to Vaska, they sounded dumb.

"Fine." Vaska's voice hardened ruthlessly. "You have your secrets, and I have mine."

"Vaska."

Vaska waved a dismissive hand at Niko as he stalked to the door. "Someone will bring you some food and a change of clothing. There's a bathroom to your left. I'll arrange a car for you when you're ready to leave."

Niko's mouth dropped open as he watched Vaska walk out of the room, the door slamming shut behind the man.

"That went well."

Niko pushed himself into a sitting position then winced when pain shot through his arms. He glanced, surprised to find white bandages around each arm. There was another white bandage, a larger one, wrapped around his chest.

Niko guessed he hadn't dreamed the fight he'd been in the night before. At least, he assumed it was the night before. He couldn't be real sure. He didn't know how long he had been unconscious.

Niko started to scoot to the edge of the bed when he heard a soft knock, and then the door swung open. A neatly dressed young man walked in carrying a breakfast tray in his hands covered with a white cloth. He smiled when he saw Niko. Niko smiled back.

"Vasiliy said you were awake and you would be hungry," the young man said as he carried the breakfast tray over and set it on the bed. He pulled the white cloth off to reveal a small plate of fresh fruit, a pastry, and a glass of orange juice. "Is there anything else I can get for you?"

"I would kill for some coffee."

"You don't have to kill for it." The man chuckled. "I can bring you up a fresh pot in a few minutes."

"I would be very grateful."

"Why don't you get started on this?" the man said. "I'll be right back with your coffee."

"Oh, wait," Niko said as the man started to walk away. "Can you tell me where I am?"

"You are at Vasiliy's estate."

"Vaska has an estate?"

"But of course." The man frowned. "Did you expect something different for Velikiy Knjaz Vasiliy Federov?"

"Velikiy Knjaz?"

"Grand Prince."

Niko started laughing as the young man walked out of the room, shutting the door behind him. Of course, that made perfect sense. Not only was he mated when he didn't want to be, but he was mated to a prince. Yep, his life was going to hell with every passing second.

Niko laughed until tears came to his eyes. He wiped them away as his laughter slowly died. He was so fucked. Vadim and Viktor would be laughing their asses off if they knew the predicament Niko had gotten himself into.

Niko's eyes strayed to his cell phone, which sat on the nightstand along with the other items that had been on him when he was attacked. Maybe calling Vadim wasn't such a bad idea. His brother might have a clue as to how to get out of this mess.

Niko grabbed his cell phone and flipped it open then dialed his brother's house. While the phone rang, Niko grabbed a piece of fresh strawberry off the plate on the breakfast tray and popped it into his mouth.

"Miroslav residence. How can I help you?"

"Mary."

"Niko?"

"Yep."

"Where are you? Your brother has been trying to reach you for days. He's worried sick."

Niko chuckled as he looked around the room he was in. One wall in the room held nothing but bookshelves full of books. They went all of the way up to the high ceiling. A stone fireplace sat on the wall opposite from the bed, two wing back chairs sitting right in front of it.

There were two solid doors on either side of the fireplace. Niko knew one led out of the room. He assumed the other led to the bathroom. That just left the French doors leading outside to the right of the bed.

There were pieces or artwork, statues, vases, and even knickknacks here and there throughout the room. There was even a large painting of…someone…over the fireplace. The painting looked old like a medieval portrait. The man in the picture looked older.

"Mary." Niko chuckled. "I have no idea where I am at the moment."

"What?"

"It's nothing really. I was attacked and knocked out. When I woke up, I was here, wherever here is."

"Niko!"

"I'm safe, Mary, I promise."

"How can you say that? You were attacked."

"It's a long story, and I'll explain it to you when I get home but at the moment, I need to talk to Vadim."

"You're coming home then?"

"Soon enough. I just have a few things I need to take care of first then I'll be home."

"I'm not liking this, Niko."

Niko laughed. "I'm not too thrilled about it either, but it is what it is at the moment."

"Niko."

"I'm fine, Mary, I promise. I just really need to talk to Vadim."

"Fine, but you'd better get home soon, or I'll be forced to call your mother."

Before Niko could reply and beg Mary not to call his mother, his call was transferred. A moment later, Niko heard his brother's voice come across the line and heaved a sigh of relief.

"Hello?"

"Vad?"

"Niko?"

"Yeah, it's me," Niko said then waited for the fallout. It wasn't long in coming. Niko popped another strawberry into his mouth and waited for his brother's tirade to finish.

"Where in the hell have you been, Niko? Mom and Dad are worried sick. You haven't been in contact in over two weeks. Don't you think it was important to check in with us? God knows what could have happened to you because we certainly didn't."

"Are you done?" Niko asked when Vadim stopped talking.

"Nikolai Miroslav, I swear to god, if you don't tell me exactly what is going on right this second, I'm going to sic Sasha on you."

Niko chuckled. "That actually might be a welcome relief."

"Why?" Vadim's voice suddenly seemed quieter, more reserved. "What's going on?"

"Vad, to tell you the truth, I'm not sure."

"Tell me what's been happening."

"Well, I haven't found a single trace of those Tri Omegas I was sent to find. In fact, as clear as I can tell, there isn't a single Tri Omega in the area, and no one has ever heard of them except in legend and lore."

"But we had reports."

"And apparently, those reports were wrong."

"So, if you can't find any Tri Omegas up there then why in the hell has it taken you so long to contact home?"

"Because there's something else going on up here. I just haven't figured out exactly what it is."

"And that kept you from calling home?"

"Uh, no, not exactly."

"Niko!"

"Have you ever heard of a man named Vasiliy Federov?"

"Yeah, sure, who hasn't?"

I haven't, Niko thought silently. "What can you tell me about him?"

"Why do you want to know?"

"I just do."

"Well, he's a couple of years older than us, so we didn't run in the same circles, but I did meet him at several wolf convocations. He seems like a nice enough guy, much better than his older brother, Ivan."

"Ivan?"

"Ivan Federov is not a man that I would like to meet in a dark alley."

"Strong?"

"No, devious. Ivan reminds me a lot of Arthur McGregor. They would be great buddies."

"Oh."

That didn't sound good to Niko. Alpha Arthur McGregor was the worst sort of alpha. He ruled his pack with an iron fist and tried to hunt down anyone that opposed him, including his son, Brom. He also hated gays with a passion.

"Hmm, I haven't met Ivan yet."

"I take it you've met Vasiliy?"

"You could say that." Niko chuckled. He felt like crying though. "I think I mated him."

Chapter 4

Vaska was sitting at the dining room table drinking coffee and reading the paper when the door opened and Niko walked in. He spared the man a quick glance to be assured there was no lasting effects from the attack the night before then went back to reading.

He couldn't understand a word. He was concentrating too hard on not letting Niko know he was concentrating on Niko. He could hear each step Niko took into the room, each breath he inhaled. He could smell Niko's sweet scent.

Vaska wanted to growl in frustration. Mates weren't supposed to deny each other, and yet that was exactly what Niko was doing. Every time Vaska thought about it, his heart stuttered in his chest. It wasn't supposed to be this way.

Mates needed each other more than they needed air. Vaska had known from the moment he smelled Niko in the bar that he had found his mate. He had been ecstatic. Vaska had been alone so long. The thought that he had finally found his mate sent waves of joy through him.

The night they had spent together had been a dream. Niko was everything Vaska had ever dreamed of and then some. Niko responded to every single touch, every kiss. Just touching the man had sent spirals of desire through Vaska.

Claiming Niko had been Vaska's greatest joy of all. Knowing that he would never be alone again, that there would always be someone by his side, it had made the load of stress Vaska was under seem miniscule.

And then the bottom had dropped out of Vaska's world. Niko didn't want him. He didn't want to be mated at all. Vaska didn't understand how the man could deny their bond once it had been established, but he wouldn't keep a man that didn't want to be there. He had more pride than that.

"Your Highness," Niko said as he approached the table. He stopped a few feet away and bowed.

Vaska frowned and snapped the paper in his hand. He didn't like the condescending tone in Niko's voice. "The proper term is Imperial Highness, Nikolai."

"My bad."

Vaska rolled his eyes when Niko scooted between him and the table and lifted himself up to sit on the polished wood. The paper was torn out of his hand and tossed on the floor then Niko moved over until he was sitting right in front of Vaska.

"It seems to me that you left out a few things, Your Imperial Highness?"

Vaska tried to control himself as he carefully set his coffee cup down on the table beside Niko. He could feel his anger and resentment starting to rise. Vaska leaned back in his chair and folded his hands together in his lap.

"What would you like to know?"

"Well," Niko scoffed, "you can start by explaining to me why you didn't tell me who you were."

"It didn't seem important at the time."

"It didn't seem important?"

"Does my being a Grand Prince mean you will accept our mating?"

"No, but—"

"Then it is not important." Vaska clenched his jaw as he reached for his coffee cup and stood to his feet. He never used his position to gain what he wanted, but if it brought him Niko, he might think about it. "I'll arrange for a car to take you back to town."

"Oh hell no, you're not getting off that easy, Vaska," Niko snapped as he jumped down off the table and grabbed Vaska's arm. "You have some explaining to do."

Vaska glared down at where Niko's hand covered his arm until the man slowly lifted it, and then he looked up at Niko. "I don't believe I have anything to explain to you, Nikolai. You've made your position more than clear."

"Vaska, you don't—"

Niko's words were interrupted by the dining room door slamming open, a young man running in. "Vasiliy, it's time."

"Very well, Markus, I'll be right there." Vaska stepped away from Niko and started for the door. "Please have a car take Nikolai back to town."

"Certainly, Vasiliy," Markus said.

"Oh no," Niko said as he raced after Vaska, "I'm not leaving until you talk."

"I don't have time for this, Nikolai."

"Then you'd better damn well make the time, Vaska."

"Nikolai."

Niko simply crossed his arms over his chest. A mutinous expression came over his face that told Vaska the man meant his words. "Fine, but it's going to have to wait until I'm done. I'll be back as soon as I can."

"So not happening." Niko shook his head. "Where you go, I go. I'm not letting you out of my sight until you talk."

"Damn it, Niko." Vaska's temper suddenly got the better of him. He grabbed Niko by his shirt and slammed him into the nearest wall. Niko's eyes were huge. "I don't have time for your fucking temper tantrum. There are some things more important than you."

"Vaska," Niko whispered.

Vaska was ashamed of his actions when he saw a flash of fear in Niko's green eyes. He never wanted his mate to be afraid of him. He just wanted Niko to understand that time was of the essence at the moment. He dropped his hands from Niko's shirt and stepped back, gesturing to him.

"Markus, see that Nikolai has anything he wants and arrange for him to have one of the guest rooms. I'll be back when I'm done."

"Yes, Vasiliy," Markus said. "I'll see to it personally."

Vaska spared Niko one last glance then hurried out of the room. He quickly made his way down the hallway to the kitchen. Only a few people knew of the secret entrance hidden away inside the kitchen pantry that led to the basement. It was better that way.

Vaska nodded to his kitchen staff, all people he trusted with his life, then made his way to the pantry. Once he shut the door behind him, he hit the hidden button that opened the secret door at the back of the pantry. The shelf of food hiding the entrance swung open, and Vaska stepped through, making sure it shut behind him.

It took him just a moment to get down the winding stone steps to the basement floor. He walked down the long stone hallway until he reached a doorway with the door open and light spilling out of it.

"Juliette, how are you feeling?" he asked as soon as he stepped inside the small room. "I understand your little one is anxious to join you."

The young woman lying on the bed nodded. Her sweat-soaked hair matted her flushed face. Her hands were clenched around the blankets beneath her. She panted heavily as a contraction rolled through her body.

Vaska rolled up his sleeves then crossed to a small bowl of water and began washing. Once he was done, he crossed over to the woman and reached for the sheet covering her body. "Well then, let's see what we can do about bringing this little one into the world."

* * * *

Vaska poured some whiskey into a small glass. He took a couple of deep gulps then added some more to the glass. Vaska rubbed the back of his neck as he carried his glass over to the window and looked out into the darkness.

It had been a long night, but luckily, both Juliette and her baby came through with flying colors. After several hours, they were sleeping peacefully downstairs in the hidden basement. Vaska knew he could safely leave them in Markus's capable hands for a few hours while he got some sleep.

"Are you ready to talk now?"

Vaska whipped around to see Niko leaning against the doorframe of his study. He breathed a sigh of relief when he saw that Niko was alone. He didn't want an audience for the argument he was sure was coming. Some things needed to be done in private.

"I don't suppose you'd wait until morning?"

"Long night?" Niko asked as he pushed away from the doorframe and walked into the room until he stood right in front of Vaska.

"You have no idea." Vaska chuckled.

"And I won't if you don't tell me."

"Niko—"

Niko held up a hand. "But I'm willing to wait until morning."

"Thank you."

"I do expect the complete truth, though."

Vaska nodded. "You'll have it."

Vaska almost protested when Niko took the whiskey out of his hand and set it on a nearby table until Niko grabbed his hand and started pulling him out of the room. "Nikolai, what are you doing?"

"You need some rest, so I'm putting you to bed."

Vaska arched an eyebrow. "You're putting me to bed?"

"Someone has to."

Vaska didn't know what to think as he followed Niko out of his study and up the stairs to his bedroom. Considering that the man refused to accept that they were mates, Niko was being very considerate.

"I am perfectly capable of putting myself to bed, Nikolai."

"Which explains oh so much why you were in your study instead of getting ready for bed."

Vaska chuckled. Niko started pulling Vaska's shirt up. Vaska grabbed the hem and held it down. "Nikolai, I appreciate your help, but I can undress myself."

Niko stepped back and crossed his arms over his chest, arching an eyebrow. "I'm waiting."

"Nikolai, I'm not going to get undressed in front of you."

"Why not?" Niko smirked. "It's not like I haven't seen the goods before."

"And you don't want the goods," Vaska snapped, all of the amusement he felt a few minutes before draining away in the blink of an eye. "That means you don't get to stand there and watch."

Vaska stormed past the astonished-looking Niko to the bedroom door. He swung it open and held onto it. "Now, I thank you for your assistance, but you can go."

"You're dismissing me?"

"No, I'm just asking you to go."

"Vaska."

"Nikolai, please, I'm tired and—"

"Why don't you call me Niko anymore?"

Vaska sighed and slammed the door closed. Niko wasn't going to leave, and he knew it. Vaska rubbed his hands over his face then dropped them down to rest them on his hips as he blew out a deep breath.

"I don't call you Niko anymore because you're not my Niko." Vaska didn't hide any of the anguish those words brought him as he turned to look at Niko. He heard the man inhale softly. "You stopped being Niko when you decided you didn't want to be my mate."

"Vaska, you don't understand."

"Then explain it to me."

"You first."

Vaska rolled his eyes then stalked across the room to the small crystal decanter on the sideboard. "I need a drink. Do you want one?"

"Is this going to be a long conversation?"

"Depends on you, I suppose."

"Then I'll take that drink."

Vaska chuckled and poured two glasses of whiskey. He carried them both over to Niko, handed him one then gestured to the chairs in front of the fireplace. "Care to join me?"

They both settled down in the chairs. Vaska took a sip of his drink as he tried to gather his thoughts. He didn't know how much to tell Niko without putting other people's lives in danger, people that depended on him.

"My brother Ivan was not a nice man."

"Was?"

Vaska nodded. "He died about six months ago."

"I'm sorry."

"I'm not. I killed him." There was something perverse in Vaska that truly enjoyed the shocked look on Niko's face. He'd bet almost anything the man hadn't expected that.

"You killed your brother?"

"Half brother, actually, but yes, I killed him." Vaska took another sip of his alcohol then stared down into the glass. "He deserved it."

"Why?"

Vaska set his whiskey down and stood. "Come with me. I want to show you something."

"Uh, okay." Niko set his glass down and stood.

Vaska led him out of the bedroom and down the stairs. There was no one in the kitchen this time when Vaska walked in and he was grateful for that. He quickly crossed to the pantry and held the door open, waiting for Niko to enter.

"The pantry?" Niko asked as he spun around. "You wanted to show me the pantry?"

"No." Vaska reached past Niko's head and hit the secret button that opened the passageway downstairs. Niko jumped when the shelf swung open.

"You have a secret passage, Vaska."

Vaska chuckled. "I do."

"Cool."

Vaska shook his head and led Niko down the stone stairs. He once again walked down the long hallway until he came to the door he'd entered just hours previously. Vaska knocked softly. A moment later the door opened, and Markus peered out.

"How is she?"

"She's resting."

"Is she awake?"

Markus smiled. "Yeah, I can't seem to get her to take her eyes off the baby."

"I'd like Juliette to meet someone."

Markus smiled and opened the door. Vaska walked past him into the room and crossed over to the bed. He sat down on the side of the bed and brushed the hair back from Juliette's face. "How are you feeling?"

"He's so beautiful, Vasiliy. I didn't think he'd ever get here."

Vaska smiled then reached down to pull the edge of the blue baby blanket back from the little angelic face. "He is very beautiful, Juliette. You did a good job."

"I couldn't have done it without you. You know neither of us would be here if it weren't for you."

"Ah, you did this all on your own. I just helped a little." Vaska gestured behind him for Niko. He saw Juliette tense when Niko walked to his side. "It's okay, this is a friend. Juliette, I'd like you to meet Nikolai Miroslav. Nikolai, my sister-in-law, Juliette Federov, and her son, Uri."

"It's a pleasure to meet you," Niko said as he nodded at Juliette.

"Likewise," Juliette said.

"He's a beautiful child," Nikolai said.

Juliette smiled, her eyes going immediately to the small child she held in her arms. "He's perfect."

"He is," Niko agreed.

Vaska stood. "We're going to let you get back to rest, Juliette, and this time I want you to actually go to sleep. You're not going to be any good to Uri if you're dead on your feet. He needs you to be in top condition."

"I just need to shift, and I should be fine."

"You can't shift for seventy-two hours, and you know it. Your body needs time to realign itself before you shift. The more rest that you get, the better shape your body will be in when you shift."

"Worrywart."

Vaska shook his finger at Juliette. "Just do what I said."

"Yes, doctor."

Vaska smiled and led Niko out of the room. He paused outside the door and looked at Markus. "Make sure she gets plenty of rest and fluids. If there are any problems, come and get me."

Markus nodded. "Could you look in on Ana real quick? She won't go to sleep."

Vaska nodded and started down the hallway again. He heard Markus close the door behind him just as he stopped and opened another door. A little girl with chestnut curls and a blanket held in her arms sat curled on one of the two beds in the room. The child on the other bed was fast asleep.

"Ana," Vaska said as he walked into the room, "what's this I hear about you not going to sleep?"

"Can't sleep," Ana said softly then immediately stuck her thumb back into her mouth.

Vaska walked across the room and sat down beside Ana on the bed. "And why not?"

"I'm waiting." The thumb in Ana's mouth came out long enough for her to talk then went right back in.

"What are you waiting for, Ana?"

"The baby." There went the thumb again.

"What about the baby, Ana?"

This time when Ana pulled her thumb from her mouth, Vaska grabbed it. Ana frowned, but answered anyway.

"You said that I could meet the baby."

Vaska wanted to bang his head against the wall. Ana remembered every damn thing anyone ever told her. "I did say that, Ana, and you will, but not until tomorrow. The baby is sleeping right now, and he needs his rest."

"But I want to meet him."

"Ana, you will get to meet Uri, I promise. But he really needs his rest. Being born takes an awful lot out of little babies like him. He is very tired right now and sleeping with Juliette."

"But—"

"Ana, you don't want Uri getting sick, do you?"

"No."

"Then he needs his rest and so do you." Vaska helped Ana lay back down on the bed then pulled the covers up to her chin. He leaned down and planted a small kiss on her forehead then tapped the tip of her nose with his finger. "Now, you go to sleep, Miss Ana. I don't want to hear another peep out of you until tomorrow."

"Yes, Vasiliy."

"Good girl." Vaska patted Ana gently then stood to his feet. He gave the other child a small look then walked to the door. Vaska clicked off the light then walked out, closing the door behind him.

When he turned, Niko was leaning against the wall giving him the strangest look. "What?" Vaska asked.

"You have kids?"

"Not exactly." Niko merely arched an eyebrow. Vaska chuckled and gestured with his hand. "Come back upstairs and I will explain everything."

"Promise?"

"Nikolai."

"I'm just saying." Niko laughed as he followed Vaska back down the hallway and up the stairs.

Vaska shook his head as they stepped back into the pantry, and the door closed behind them, once again hiding the secret passage. He tapped the pantry shelf with his hand. "Very few people know of this passage, Nikolai, and I would like to keep it that way."

"Understood."

Vaska seriously doubted it, but Niko would know soon enough how important it was to keep the secret passage a secret. Vaska opened the pantry door and walked right into Andrei, the last man he wanted to see.

"Andrei."

"Having fun in the pantry, Vasiliy?"

Vaska's heart froze in his chest. Andrei had been the beta and best friend of Vaska's brother, Ivan. The man was nearly as bad as Ivan. The only reason Vaska hadn't gotten rid of him already was because he couldn't prove Andrei had done anything wrong.

"Actually, we were," Niko said from behind him. "Do you have a problem with that?"

Fear spiraled through Vaska's chest when Niko stepped forward and Andrei spotted him. It was a fear that Vaska had only felt once before in his life, the night he heard Niko get attacked then found him beaten and passed out in the street.

"Who are you?"

Vaska didn't miss the quickening of Andrei's breathing when the man's eyes moved up and down Niko's body. Vaska growled when Andrei's arousal filled the room. Niko might not want to be mated to him, but Vaska was still his mate. That meant no other men.

"I'm Nikolai. Who are you?"

"Andrei, and it's a pleasure to meet you."

"Pleasure to meet you, too, Andrei, but if you'll excuse us, Vaska and I need to take this party upstairs."

It wasn't until Niko passed by him that Vaska understood what had Andrei in a dither. Niko's shirt was unbuttoned and hanging out of his pants, and those had the top two buttons open. His hair was mussed, and he looked recently kissed.

Niko was a walking wet dream.

Vaska just didn't understand why Niko looked like that. He'd been with the man all the way from upstairs and no one had kissed Niko. Vaska would have noticed, and then he would have killed whoever was kissing Niko.

"Is this an open party or invitation only?" Andrei asked as they walked past him.

"Sorry," Niko said. "I don't share."

"Too bad."

Vaska growled. He couldn't help himself. Andrei was looking at Niko like he was a piece of prized candy. Vaska didn't want anyone looking at Niko like that. He grabbed Niko by his arm and pushed him through the kitchen.

"Goodnight, Andrei."

Chapter 5

Niko could barely walk by the time they reached Vaska's room. He was laughing too hard. The look on Andrei's face when he was turned down had been hilarious. The look on Vaska's face when he saw Niko's unbuttoned shirt and pants had been better.

"Just who is that guy?" Niko asked as Vaska walked in behind him and shut the bedroom door.

"That was Andrei Sakharov. He was my brother's beta."

"He's a creep." Niko gave a full-body shudder.

"Yes, I've often thought so."

"I thought he was going to hump my leg there for a minute."

"He might not have if you hadn't stripped in front of him."

Niko swung around and gaped at Vaska. "I didn't strip."

"You might as well have." Vaska waved his hand up and down Niko's body. "Just look at you."

"Why should I?" Niko snapped as he planted his hands on his hips. "You're doing enough looking for me."

"Nikolai!" Vaska exclaimed.

"Vaska!" Niko exclaimed right back.

Vaska groaned loudly as he rubbed his hands down his face. "Maybe it's a good thing you won't accept our mating. You'd drive me crazy in a week."

Niko's eyes narrowed as he watched Vaska walk over and sit down in one of the chairs in front of the fireplace. Vaska grabbed the glass off the table and started drinking from it. The more Vaska mentioned Niko's refusal to accept their mating, the less Niko liked it. It rankled somehow.

"It wasn't like I asked the guy to join us, Vaska. I was just trying to give Andrei a reason for us being in the pantry."

"Oh, you did that all right." Vaska snickered sarcastically. "I imagine right now Andrei is jerking off in his bathroom fantasizing about what we were doing in the pantry."

"One, eewww." Niko held up one finger then another. "And two, isn't what I did better than him finding your little secret passage? I thought you wanted to keep it a secret?"

"Displaying your body for everyone to see is never better, Nikolai," Vaska said. "You never should have done it."

"That's not up to you."

"No," Vaska snapped, "because my fucking mate doesn't want me."

Niko jerked in shock when Vaska jumped to his feet and threw his glass into the fireplace. The sounds of glass shattering and flames hissing filled the room. Niko swallowed hard as Vaska seemed to fold into himself right before his eyes.

"Vaska," he whispered.

"You should go back to your room now, Nikolai," Vaska said very quietly as he watched the flames sputter. He almost seemed surprised at his loss of control. "We can talk tomorrow."

"Vaska."

"Please, Nikolai. We'll talk in the morning."

Niko pressed his lips together to keep from arguing. He had a lot more he wanted to say to Vaska, but maybe now wasn't the time. Vaska really did look upset, and Niko knew he was the reason.

"I guess I'll see you in the morning then."

Vaska didn't make a sound or in any way try to stop Niko as he walked out of the room. Niko waited for a moment outside of the bedroom, hoping Vaska might come after him. When he didn't, Niko slowly walked down the hallway to his room. The need to go back and comfort Vaska grew with each step Niko took away from the man.

Niko was realistic about who he was. He didn't make commitments, and he didn't stick around for seconds. He was a "fuck 'em and leave 'em" type of guy. Which was why this need he felt to comfort Vaska confused Niko so much.

Niko almost turned and went back to Vaska's room when he reached his door. Then he remembered Vaska's softly spoken words when he asked Niko to leave. Vaska had been very upset. Niko didn't think he would be welcomed if he came back. Maybe it was time to really think about leaving.

Niko groaned as he remembered yet another thing. Vaska was supposed to explain what in the hell was going on in the morning. Niko had enough of a curiosity to want to hear that explanation. But he could always leave after that.

Shaking his head, Niko opened the guest bedroom and stepped inside. He skidded to a stop before he'd even let go of the door handle. The sight before him was definitely one Niko hadn't been expecting.

"Andrei, what are you doing in my room?"

The naked man spread out on his bed chuckled. "I've come to see if we could have our own little party, of course."

"I'm not in the mood to party, thanks."

Andrei's lower lip came out, and Niko knew the man thought it was cute. Niko wasn't of the same mind. He still found Andrei creepy. Still, he was shocked when Andrei rolled over onto his hands and knees and wiggled his ass.

"I know Vasiliy didn't let you fuck him. He doesn't do that." Andrei winked over his shoulder. "But I do. I'll let you have my ass."

Niko shivered. He felt like a cold shiver moved over his body. "No, thank you."

Andrei plopped down on his side and bent one knee, spreading his legs and grabbing his cock. "I can do a lot more for you than Vasiliy can," he said as he stroked himself.

"I don't care what you can do, Andrei." Niko pointed to the hallway. "I want you to leave."

Andrei pouted again. "Now, don't be like that, Nikolai. We could have a really good time together. I can give you whatever Vasiliy can and then some. I know how to treat a man like a man."

"What is this fixation you have on Vaska?" Niko asked as he waved his hands in an exasperated motion. "Why are you so obsessed with him?"

"Vaska?" Andrei suddenly sat up. The pouty look left his face. "You call him Vaska?"

"Yeah." Niko frowned. "Don't you?"

Niko's heart stuttered with fear when Andrei suddenly shifted into his wolf form and lunged off the bed. Niko jumped back but not in enough time. Andrei came down on top of him, crashing them both to the floor.

Niko winced when Andrei's claws sank into his sides. He couldn't pull them away though. He was too busy wrapping his hands around Andrei's furry neck, keeping the wolf's sharp canine teeth away from his throat.

Andrei was snarling and growling. He kept lunging at Niko as if trying to break free of the hold Niko had on his neck. Niko could see madness and a desire for blood in Andrei's eyes and knew the man wanted to kill him.

He couldn't shift to defend himself. In the split second it would take to shift, Andrei could kill him. Niko did the only thing he could think of doing considering the situation. He shouted for Vaska through their mating bond.

"Vaska!"

* * * *

Vaska's head exploded. He dropped the glass in his hand and grabbed his head. When the pounding slowed down to a dull thud and

Vaska could think again, he realized that Niko had used their mating bond to call him.

"Niko?"

"I need help!"

Vaska was up out of his chair and running down the hallway before Niko even finished speaking. His heart hammered in his chest when he reached Niko's room and looked inside. Andrei was in wolf form and had Niko pinned to the floor. It was obvious from the snarling and lunges that Andrei was trying to kill Niko.

Vaska didn't need to know what happened. He didn't even care if Niko had started the fight. Someone was trying to kill his mate. That's all that mattered to Vaska. He shifted into his wolf form as he ran through the doorway.

Vaska used all of his strength and speed to smash into Andrei and drag him off of Niko. They crashed to the floor several feet away from Niko. Vaska spared a quick glance at his mate to assure himself he was safe. When he saw Niko shifting into his wolf form, Vaska returned his attention to Andrei.

He had Andrei pinned to the floor, but the wolf was fighting back for all he was worth. Vaska could feel Andrei's claws digging into his sides and knew he'd have some deep gashes by the time this was done.

He was still determined to win. No one was going to go after his mate and not pay the price. Vaska lunged forward and snapped his teeth at Andrei. He could feel blood and fur in his mouth and knew he'd gotten a piece of Andrei, but it wasn't enough.

Vaska snarled and snapped at Andrei again with his teeth. He got air this time when Andrei kicked out with his back feet at the exact same time, hitting Vaska in the stomach. Vaska fell back on the floor with a yelp then quickly scrambled to get to his feet when he saw Andrei's attention turn toward Niko.

His feet slid on the hardwood floor. Vaska's heart started to pound faster when he couldn't gain any ground. He just kept sliding on the slick polished wood. Vaska dropped down to all fours. He slowly stood to his feet and dug his claws into the floor.

Once he knew he could move without sliding, Vaska started across the floor again, running faster and faster with each step. Andrei and Niko were struggling furiously, rolling around on the floor as each one of them tried to gain the dominant position.

Vaska tried to jump in and attack Andrei, but every time he did, Andrei would turn and Niko would be in front of him. And he couldn't attack Niko, no matter how mad he was at the man.

Vaska went for Andrei's legs instead. He started running then crouched down until he slid into Andrei's legs, knocking him to the floor. Vaska was on Andrei in a split second, clamping his jaws around the wolf's throat.

Andrei tried to struggle away, clawing at Vaska's chest. Vaska just bit down harder until Andrei whimpered and the fight drained out of him. Vaska held on for a moment longer then slowly released his hold on Andrei's throat.

"Shift, Andrei."

Vaska turned to see Niko standing beside him in human form. He had a few scrapes and scratches on him, but other than that, Niko looked to be fine. Vaska moved over to stand between Andrei and Niko, growling at the wolf still lying on the floor.

"I'd shift if I were you, Andrei. Vaska doesn't seem to be in a very accommodating mood."

Andrei's shift was slow, telling Vaska that he had injured the man. He couldn't say he was sorry. It had been his intention to injure the man. Once Andrei had fully shifted to human form, Vaska followed. He stood to his feet, making sure he stayed between Andrei and Niko, then asked the one question floating in his head.

"Why, Andrei?"

"You took what was mine. I was taking what was yours. A simple eye for an eye."

Vaska frowned. "I never took anything of yours."

Andrei pushed himself to his feet, glaring at Vaska the entire time. Vaska could see the hatred in Andrei's eyes. He just didn't know why he hadn't seen it before. Hatred that deep didn't happen overnight. This had been building for some time.

"You took Ivan from me."

"Ivan was never yours, Andrei. He had a mate."

"Juliette was not Ivan's mate. I was. Ivan said I was."

"Is that why you and Ivan killed her?" Vaska heard Niko's soft inhale as he spoke and hoped the man would keep his mouth shut. No one needed to know that Juliette was alive right now.

"She deserved to die," Andrei snapped. "She tried to keep Ivan from me."

"She was his mate!"

"She was his whore!"

"She was the mother of his child."

Andrei's grin was cruel and filled with malice. "Not anymore."

Vaska slowly shook his head and took a couple of steps back. He felt the sudden need to be closer to Niko, to protect him. "You're insane."

"Am I?"

Before Vaska could answer Andrei and tell the man what he really thought of him, a loud blaring alarm filled the air.

"What now?" Vaska shouted, growing frustrated by the second. He really needed to get some sleep, and no one seemed to be making it easy for him.

A chill of foreboding ran down Vaska's spine when Andrei laughed hysterically then made a mad dash for the French doors. He crashed through them and ran into the darkness before Vaska could stop him.

"Fuck!" Vaska shouted to the ceiling. He so did not need this.

"Vaska, what in the hell is that alarm?"

Vaska dropped his head back on his shoulders and squeezed his eyes closed for a moment. "It's the damn perimeter alarm."

"But it went off before Andrei took off."

Vaska's eyes snapped open as he realized Niko was right. "Shit!"

"Vaska, what's going on?"

"Come with me," he shouted as he ran out of the room and made his way back to his bedroom. He quickly shut the door as soon as Niko ran through then made his way over to the fireplace.

One quick press of a couple of strategically placed stones and the fire burning inside the fireplace died down and the back of the fireplace swung open. Niko bent down to look inside and gasped.

"You have secret passages all over the place, Vaska."

"This is a very old house."

"This is a very cool house."

Vaska grinned at the excitement he could hear in Niko's voice. He just hoped the man was as excited when he discovered the need for the secret passages. "Follow me."

Vaska ducked inside the large fireplace then waited for Niko to step through. Once he had, Vaska hit another series of stones and the fireplace door closed. Vaska turned and started walking down the cold stone passageway.

"I discovered these passageways when I was a small boy. I used to play in them for hours, usually when I was trying to hide from my father and my brother. They were two very like-minded people."

"Oh?"

"My father believed that the pack was there for him. He didn't understand that he was there for the pack."

"I've heard this story before."

"My brother was the same way. He took what he wanted when he wanted. He paid no attention to his duties as my father's heir and later as alpha of the pack. As long as he got his way, he was happy. If anyone tried to resist him, they were eliminated."

"Yep," Niko said, "I've definitely heard this story before."

Vaska grimaced. "It seems to be a very popular theme."

"A lot of people are in power that shouldn't be."

"I agree, but until the Wolf Council moves into the current century, we're pretty much on our own here."

"Is that why you killed your brother?"

Vaska stopped walking and glanced back at Niko. "No, I killed Ivan because he was trying to kill Juliette."

"He tried to kill his mate? Wait, I thought you said Andrei tried to kill Juliette."

Niko sounded horrified, which was just how Vaska had felt when he came upon Ivan trying to strangle Juliette. Vaska didn't much like his brother, but he hadn't wanted to kill him. He did it to save Juliette and her unborn child.

"There has been more than one attempt on Juliette's life. We now know why Andrei tried to kill her. Ivan tried to kill Juliette because he discovered that she was pregnant and, apparently, that was unacceptable to him."

"But a cub is to be loved and cherished, each one a gift. How could he try and kill a child?"

Niko's face had paled. His eyes looked agonized. He looked so upset that Vaska couldn't prevent himself from wrapping an arm around Niko's shoulders and giving him a quick hug. He didn't know how else to comfort the man.

"Unfortunately, not everyone believes as you do, Nikolai."

"I would never harm a child," Niko whispered.

"Nor would I, Nikolai, which is why I had to kill my brother."

Vaska was surprised when Niko tilted his head back to look up at him then stroked the side of his ace. "I'm sorry, Vaska. You shouldn't have had to go through that."

Vaska smiled, warmed by Niko's concern. "Thank you, Nikolai. That means a lot coming from you."

Niko's eyes dropped to Vaska's mouth. He licked his lips then his eyes flickered back up. "I never meant to be such a pain in the ass, Vaska. As beta to the Vourdala pack, I've seen a lot of things, some good, some not so good. It makes me wary of any type of commitment."

"It terrifies the hell out of me," Vaska admitted.

"Yeah." Niko chuckled. He sounded nervous and breathless all at the same time. "But maybe we should talk about—"

Vaska quickly pressed his hand over Niko's mouth. "Why don't you hold that thought until after we find out why the perimeter alarm went off?"

Niko nodded.

Vaska slid his hand away from Niko's mouth and moved it up to hold the side of his face. Vaska took a chance and grabbed a quick kiss from Niko. When the man didn't protest but leaned into him, Vaska took the kiss deeper.

This kiss, unlike their previous passion-filled ones, was slow and sweet. Vaska purposefully licked at Niko's upper lip and felt him open up. He swept his tongue inside and brushed it back and forth, slowly, then reluctantly pulled away and held Niko's face gently in his hands.

"We will talk about this, majiktoka, this and everything else. I promise."

Niko smirked. "I've heard that before, too."

"Just keep believing me for a little while longer, Nikolai, please."

Niko nodded.

"Come on, we'd better get going," Vaska said as he started down the passageway again. "Whatever set off the alarms isn't going to wait for us."

"Do your alarms go off often?"

"Not that often, but it does happen."

"Could it be one of your pack?"

Vaska paused and glanced over his shoulder. "Nikolai, I don't have a pack."

Niko's forehead wrinkled. "But, I thought…what about Markus and Juliette and the little demon?"

"The little demon?"

Niko rolled his eyes. "The little girl with chestnut curls."

Vaska chuckled and started walking again. "Little demon does kind of describe her, doesn't it?"

"Have you heard the lungs on that child? She could shatter steel."

"Well, do me favor, don't call her that. She's been called enough things in her life. That's why she's here. Her pack killed her parents when they were trying to take her. She's had enough bad things happen in her life."

"Vaska, I would never call a child any name. I only said it because it's just the two of us in here. I'd never even say it if someone else was with us."

"I'm not sure I'd say it even then. Ana could hear you."

"Vaska," Niko scoffed, "we're in a stone passageway on the second floor. Ana is in the basement. How in the hell is she going to hear me?"

"Ana is a Tri Omega, Nikolai," Vaska said. "Everyone in the basement is."

Chapter 6

Niko stared at Vaska, not realizing he'd stopped walking until the man took several steps away from him. He had a good excuse though. He was in complete shock.

"Vaska, I was sent here to find a pack of Tri Omegas."

"I know," Vaska said without turning around.

"You know?" Niko hurried to catch up. "Wait, you know?"

"Why do you think I went to the bar the night we met? I received word that someone was asking questions, and I needed to find out who it was. I wasn't expecting you, however."

"Why haven't you said anything to me?"

"I've been trying to, but we keep getting off track or getting interrupted."

Niko's mind reeled. He couldn't seem to land on any single thought. Vaska and the people in the basement could be the answer to everything he'd been searching for. His mission might be over in a matter of days.

That thought didn't bring Niko any pleasure. It might mean leaving Vaska, and Niko wasn't quite ready to do that yet. He was starting to really like the guy. And being mated to the man was starting to not look so horrifying.

Niko followed Vaska down a set of stone circular stairs. They reminded him of a medieval staircase from a castle. Grey stoned walls lined each side of the staircase and torches lit the way. It was weird and creepy at the same time.

When they reached the bottom, the hallway opened into a small room. There were boxes stacked in every corner. The room reminded

Niko of a storage pantry. The labels for dry goods and supplies on the sides of the boxes confirmed that belief.

There just didn't seem to be an exit.

"Um, Vaska?"

"Yes?"

"Where's the door?" Niko asked as he looked around. There wasn't a door or window in sight. "How do we get out of here?"

"Magic."

Niko arched and eyebrow and watched Vaska walk over to one of the walls. After the last two secret passages, Niko was in no way surprised when Vaska turned one of the torch holders and a wall slid back, revealing another passage.

"This place is full of surprises, isn't it?"

"Like I said, it's a very old house."

Niko hurried forward when Vaska gestured to him then watched as the man closed the secret door in the wall. Once the wall slid back in place, it looked like it had been there for hundreds of years. No one would know it was a secret door.

"That is so freaky."

"*That* is useful," Vaska replied. "It's helped me keep all of these people safe for the last few months."

"Safe from what?"

"Other wolf packs that want to use them for their own purposes, relatives that think they are freaks and need to be put to death, human hunters that want a wolf pelt." Vaska shrugged. "Take your pick."

"But why you?" Niko asked. "Why have you been keeping them safe?"

"Someone had to."

"What about the council?"

"They are part of the problem."

"The council?"

"Nikolai, you have to understand about Tri Omegas, they—"

Niko held up his hand. "I know all about Tri Omegas, Vaska. I know several. In fact, my best friend is mated to one."

"You're talking about Viktor Stylianos, aren't you?"

"Yeah." Niko frowned. "How did you know?"

"I made it my business to know. Once I knew we had mated, I still had to be sure I could trust you before I told you anything about my life. Too many people depend on me. While you were unconscious from that attack, I made a few phone calls."

"Did you find out what you wanted?" Niko rankled a little at being investigated by his mate but not enough to make an issue of it. He could understand where Vaska was coming from. Not everyone got the mate of their dreams.

"I did. I found out that my mate is someone that not only I can trust, but he is an honorable man." Vaska grinned. "He's also damn cute."

"Geez, who did you talk to, my mother?"

"I have a friend that works for the Eastern European Council. While I don't trust the council itself, I do trust him."

Niko arched an eyebrow, a sudden possessiveness flashing through him. "Do you trust this *friend* more than you trust me?"

"Siro? No. We've just spent some time fighting on the same lines together."

"Is he someone I need to be concerned about?" Niko almost slapped his hand over his mouth when Vaska glanced back at him in surprise. He didn't know where his words were coming from. Niko shook his head and waved his hand in Vaska's direction. "Ignore me. I have no idea where that came from."

"I do." Vaska chuckled. "But not to worry, Nikolai, I'll explain it to you later."

Niko rolled his eyes as Vaska laughed. They both froze when a door down the hallway opened until they saw Markus peek out. Niko followed after Vaska when he hurried down the hallway.

"What happened?" Markus asked. "What's going on?"

"The perimeter alarm has been tripped, Markus."

"And Andrei attacked us then ran off," Niko added. He felt it was important that Markus know about Andrei. Markus was allowed in the secret basement. Andrei was not. That had to mean something.

"Andrei attacked you?" Markus glanced over his shoulder for a moment then looked back. "Does he know about Juliette?"

"No, he still thinks he killed her," Vaska said. "However, he did try to kill Niko because I killed Ivan, something about an eye for an eye. Andrei is convinced that he was Ivan's mate, not Juliette."

"He's nuts!" Markus hissed.

"Yeah, that's what I told him," Vaska said. "He escaped when the alarm went off."

"He didn't set the alarm off?"

Vaska shook his head. "No, and I don't know who did. I was just getting ready to go check, but I wanted to bring Nikolai down here first. Nikolai's going to protect you all while I go investigate the alarm. I want you to do whatever he says, understand?"

"Of course, Vasiliy."

"Nikolai is my mate, Markus. He stands in my stead."

Niko gaped at Vaska, astonished at the trust the man was giving him. He was also a little concerned with the amount of responsibility that Vaska was putting in his hands. Niko was a beta for a reason. He didn't like responsibility.

"There's one more thing, Markus. If anything happens to me, I want you to help Nikolai get everyone back to his pack."

"Vaska, no!" Niko's heart started to pound frantically. "Nothing is going to happen to you."

Vaska turned around and grabbed Niko by the arms, not tightly but just enough to hold him still. "Nikolai, we can't know that. We have no idea who tripped the alarm."

"Then stay down here. We can all hide together."

"I wish I could, Nikolai, but someone has to find out what is going on."

"Why does it have to be you?"

"Because there is no one else to do it."

Niko didn't like that answer. He didn't like it at all. Vaska shouldn't have to be trying to hide all of these people by himself. He needed someone in his corner, and it looked like that someone was going to be Niko.

Who knew?

"Fine, go do what you have to do." Niko shook his finger at Vaska. "But remember, you owe me an explanation. I fully expect to get one when you get back, so you'd better make sure your ass comes back."

"As you decree, Nikolai, so shall it be."

Niko blinked for a moment. "And don't you forget it, prince."

"Grand Prince, Nikolai."

"Whatever."

Vaska cocked his head to one side, a peculiar expression on his face. "I see my title isn't going to get me very far with you, is it?"

"Not really." Niko shrugged. "Maybe if you were a duke or something, it might."

A bit of laughter burst from Vaska's lips. "Nikolai, a duke is below a prince in title ranking."

"Yeah, but can you imagine? If we stay together I'd be a princess." Niko shuddered. "My brother and Viktor would never let me live that down."

"And duchess is better?"

"No, not really." Niko grimaced. He hadn't thought of that. "Maybe we can just dump the title all together."

"If it makes you feel any better, I don't like the title much either. I only got it because Ivan was dead and I was next in line to inherit the title. I'm not prince or duke material."

"So, save it for Uri then."

Vaska seemed to blink for a moment then he laughed. "I think that's one of the best ideas you've had yet."

"Yeah, I'm full of them." In fact, Niko had an idea that he thought was better than letting Uri inherit Vaska's title. He wanted to call in reinforcements. He was tired of people attacking him and Vaska, and he knew just the people to help him keep them both safe.

"You go do whatever it is you need to do," Niko said as he reached into his pocket and pulled out his cell phone. "I have something I need to do as well."

"Who are you calling, Nikolai?" Vaska asked. "You know these people's lives depend on keeping them secret."

"Not to worry, Vaska. I won't mention them at all." Niko dialed his brother then held the phone to his ear as he waited for the man to come on the line. "Vad? It's me," Niko said as soon as he heard his brother's voice. "How do you feel about attending a little mating celebration in the wilds of Russia?"

* * * *

Niko rubbed his hands on his pant legs and tried not to let his nails dig into his palms as he paced back and forth in the hallway. Vaska had been gone for nearly twenty minutes, and the waiting was driving Niko crazy.

The alarm stopped blaring about ten minutes after Vaska left. Niko didn't know what that meant. Down in the basement surrounded by earth and stone, Niko also couldn't hear anything except the sound of his own breathing. Well, his and the other people in the basement.

"Vasiliy will be okay."

Niko swung around to see Markus leaning against one of the doorframes. "You think so?"

"He is a strong one. He's been taking care of himself and us for quite some time."

"Vaska said that he's only been in charge for about six months."

"True." Markus nodded. "But he's been taking care of us in one form or another for a lot longer than that."

"He seems to be pretty good at it."

"He is. He's a doctor, you know?"

Niko blinked. "No, actually, I didn't know that."

Markus nodded then pushed away from the doorframe. "Come with me. I want to introduce you to a few people."

Curiosity ate at Niko, and he followed quickly behind Markus. They walked down the hallway to another door, one Niko hadn't been in before. Markus opened the door and walked right on in. Niko paused at the door and looked inside.

Three people sat in the small room. A young man about nineteen or so sat playing cards at a wooden table. Two younger boys, Niko guessed around five and eight, sat reading books on a small twin-sized bed.

"Boys, I want you to meet a friend."

All three boys looked up. Niko caught a trace of fear in their eyes before they quickly masked it. He didn't know their story, but he knew it hadn't been a good one. These boys were clearly afraid for their lives.

"Niko, this is Jonathan, Steven, and William," Markus said.

"Hello." Niko nodded at each of them. They still didn't say a word, just watched Niko warily.

"This is Niko, Vasiliy's mate."

The mention of Vaska's name seemed to make a great deal of difference in the boys' demeanor. Their stiff posture loosened and small smiles broke out over their lips. Niko smiled back and tried not to look intimidating.

"It's nice to meet you all."

"Are you really Vasiliy's mate?" the smallest boy asked.

"It would seem so, yes," Niko replied.

"Jonathan, Steven, and William are three of the boys in our little program here," Markus said as he gestured to them. "Jonathan came to us about three months ago, smuggled in by some fishermen from

England. Steve and William actually made it here on their own. It took them almost four months, but they made it."

"By themselves?" Niko gasped. "But where are their parents? Their pack?"

"Mom and Dad were killed," the older of the two boys said. "Our alpha tried to take us from them, and they put up a fight. Mom hid us before they killed her. She said for us to come here once everyone was gone."

"Just how many people know about Vasiliy?" Niko suddenly worried for Vaska's safety more than he did a second before. His mate wasn't just trying to save people. People were coming to him because they knew about him. That put Vaska in more danger.

"We have a kind of Tri Omega underground," Markus said. "There are safe houses set up all over the world. Each safe house only knows about the next one on the road to here. They don't know where the people come from or where the other safe houses are, just the next one in the line. When a Tri Omega comes to them, they feed them, care for them, and send them on to the next safe house until they reach us."

"It's because of how many Tri Omegas are being born, isn't it?"

Markus nodded. "In ancient times, only one Tri Omega was born per generation. When one was born, he or she would be turned over to the Wolf Council to be raised. They were celebrated, almost worshipped. They were protected and allowed to develop their powers for the greater good of all the wolf packs."

"And now?"

"Too many are being born. That's thrown the entire system out of balance. Packs are keeping their Tri Omegas hidden away, keeping them virtual prisoners. That is assuming that they don't try and kill them first for being freaks."

"Killing them?" Niko gasped. "How could they even consider killing them?"

"Like I said, packs have been hiding their Tri Omegas. It's been so long since most packs have actually seen a Tri Omega that people have forgotten what they are. They've fallen into legend, a myth. No one believes they actually exist."

"Oh, I can assure you they do." Niko snorted. "I've met quite a few."

"You know other Tri Omegas?" Jonathan asked.

Niko nodded. "I do. My best friend is mated to one, and I have a few other friends that have Tri Omegas as mates."

"Have they found their other mates?"

Niko smiled. "They have. Each triad is very happy."

"Wow." Jonathan leaned back in his chair, staring off into space. "I can't wait to meet my mates."

"Just remember that you need both of them," Niko said. "Don't let one of them claim you before you find them both. That happened to my friend, Ryland. He didn't know he was a Tri Omega and let one of his mates claim him before he found his other one. It was only by chance that Ryland and Gregory found Viktor."

"Yeah, Vasiliy explained the rules to us." Jonathan nodded. "We can't shift until we find both of our mates, and our powers only come in after we are claimed. We need both of our mates to survive, keep us grounded."

"You also need to remember that once you have found both of your mates they have to claim you quite often, no less than every couple of days. If they don't, you could die."

Jonathan frowned. "But, Juliette didn't die."

"Juliette is a Tri Omega, too?" Niko asked as he turned to look at Markus. He was confused when Markus nodded. "But how is she still alive then?"

"We don't know. Unfortunately, we didn't know at the time Vasiliy killed Ivan that Juliette was a Tri Omega. We only found out afterwards."

"Actually, that might explain a lot. Andrei kept going on and on about how he was Ivan's mate. He could have been telling the truth. Maybe Ivan, Andrei, and Juliette were all mated to each other."

"Niko, that still doesn't explain how Juliette is still alive if one of her mates has died."

"Did Ivan bite her?"

Markus shrugged. "I would assume so. He got her pregnant."

"That doesn't mean he bit her. You might want to ask her."

"Well, we know for sure that Andrei never claimed her."

"No, we don't," Niko replied. "Vaska told me that Andrei tried to kill Juliette. If he bit her during the scuffle, then she might have been claimed by both her mates, assuming Ivan also claimed her."

"If you you're right, that still doesn't explain why Juliette is still alive."

"Nope, but I think figuring that out needs to be one of our top priorities."

"Fuck!" Markus exclaimed as he pushed his hand through his sandy blond hair. "We need a damn how-to manual."

"Why do you think I'm here?" Niko snickered. "We've had so many problems with our Tri Omegas, we thought finding out everything we could about them and writing it all down in a book would be our best bet. We've come too close to losing too many of them."

"That's why you're here?" Jonathan asked. "I thought it was because you were Vasiliy's mate."

"It's a long story but sufficient to say, my alpha sent me up here to do some investigating because we had heard that there was an entire pack of Tri Omegas living here. I did not expect to find Vaska. That was just a bonus for me."

"Does Vasiliy know why you're here?" Jonathan asked.

Niko could hear the concern and need to protect Vaska in Jonathan's voice and felt that it pointed to what type of man Vaska was that he had someone so worried about him. "Yes, Vaska is perfectly aware of why I am here. In fact, he's already had me investigated to make sure I was trustworthy." Niko spread his hands and grinned. "I'm still here."

"Vasiliy also personally told me that Niko is in charge in his stead," Markus said. "I believe that Vasiliy trusts Niko, and I think you should too."

The boys nodded, even if they still looked wary, and Niko was grateful for that. It would be hard to work with these people and keep them safe if they were afraid of Niko. He also realized that the quicker Vaska came back and reassured them, the better.

"Just how many Tri Omegas are there here?" he asked.

"Well, there's Juliette and her baby, the boys here, Ana and her brother, and Antonio."

"Antonio?"

Markus gestured with his hand and walked out of the room. Niko waved to the boys then followed Markus out of the room and down the hallway. Markus stopped outside the room next to Juliette's. He opened the door slowly and peered inside then gestured to Niko to join him.

Niko frowned and walked up to the door. He peaked around the edge and searched the room until he spotted a small bundle huddled in the corner by the bottom of the bed. Whoever it was had the blanket pulled up over their head. The only reason Niko even knew someone was there was from the slight up-and-down motion under the blanket from someone breathing.

He arched an eyebrow at Markus and watched him quietly close the door. "What's wrong with him?"

"Antonio was badly dehydrated when he arrived here and bordering on starvation. The only person he will even acknowledge is Vasiliy. He doesn't scream anymore when I come in to feed him or treat his wounds but—"

"Wounds?"

"He was beaten severely, whipped right down to the bone." Markus grimaced. "For awhile there, I thought we were going to lose him, but Vasiliy pulled him through. Antonio's body is healing, but his spirit"—Markus shook his head—"I'm not sure it ever will."

"Do you know who beat him?"

"No, he won't tell us, but Vasiliy suspects his pack. Every time Vasiliy tries to get Antonio to talk about his pack or where he's from, Antonio goes into hysterics, and we have to sedate him. I'm not sure we'll ever know."

"I don't understand why these Tri Omegas are being treated like they are. Even normal pack members wouldn't be treated this way. Tri Omegas are extra special. They deserve better care than this."

"I'm glad you think so, majiktoka," said a voice from behind Niko. "We may need your strength in the coming days."

Niko swung around then inhaled sharply when he took in Vaska's condition. He looked like he had been in a battle for his life, his clothing torn and bloody, open, bleeding wounds marring much of his exposed skin.

"Vaska," he shouted as he ran forward, catching the man right before he crashed to the floor. He slowly lowered Vaska to the cold stone tiles then sat down and leaned back against the wall so he could cradle the man in his arms.

"What happened, Vaska?"

"I came back to you, majiktoka."

Niko gently brushing the sweat-matted hair back from Vaska's bruised face. He sniffled and tried to hold back the tears unexpectedly brimming in his eyes. "You did, Vaska, and I'm very grateful. I don't want to lose my mate just when I found him."

Chapter 7

Vaska stretched his arms over his head and wiggled his toes. It felt good to stretch out. He suddenly opened his eyes and sat up and leaned back on his arms as he realized that he was awake...and unhurt. Not an inch of his body was in pain, and it should have been after the battle he fought the night before.

At least, he assumed it was the night before.

"Go back to sleep, honey."

Vaska jolted when he heard the mumbled words and felt a hand gently pat his hip. He glanced down to find Niko curled up in bed beside him. Niko's eyes were closed, and he seemed to be pretty much asleep. Vaska also noticed that Niko was naked.

Vaska scooted back down on the bed and rolled to his side until he faced Niko. He ran his hand lightly along Niko's side, pressing his lips together to keep from chuckling when Niko squirmed and tried to push into his light touch.

Niko was very responsive to Vaska's touch, and Vaska loved that. He just had to touch the man or kiss him, and Niko was running on a hundred and twenty percent lust. It was a heady feeling knowing he could ramp his mate up so much.

And Niko was his mate. The man had admitted as much the night before. Vaska was positive of that. It wasn't something he would forget no matter how injured he'd been at the time. Niko was his, and Vaska wasn't going to let the man go now that he had him.

"Majiktoka," Vaska whispered then blew across Niko's face.

Niko wiggled his nose then snuggled his face back into the pillow. Vaska chuckled silently and blew again. Niko swiped at his face with his hand, grumbled, and pushed back into the pillow.

"Majiktoka," Vaska whispered again. "Waky, waky."

Niko's sleepy eyes suddenly popped open and looked at Vaska. "Waky, waky? Really?"

Vaska grinned. Niko rolled over onto his back and rubbed his eyes. When he dropped his hands to his chest and glared, Vaska chuckled at the disgruntled look in Niko's green eyes.

"You're not a morning person, are you?"

"Only if I'm still up from the night before," Niko said.

"But mornings are so wonderful, majiktoka," Vaska said as he scooted closer to Niko's body and started stroking his hands over the man's hairless chest. "The morning sun is shining through the windows, the countryside is waking up." Vaska leaned in and scraped his tongue across Niko's nipple. "It's just the two of us."

Niko inhaled and arched. "Yeah, I see what you mean."

Vaska grinned at the lust he could suddenly see burning in Niko's eyes. "I thought you might."

"Wait." Niko grabbed Vaska's hand. "Are you feeling okay?"

"I don't know. Why don't you feel me and find out."

Niko arched an eyebrow. "You're really weird in the morning."

"Does that mean you don't want to feel me?"

"No, it doesn't, but could you have chosen a worse pickup line?"

"Give me a few minutes." Vaska chuckled. "I'm sure I can amaze you even more."

Vaska leaned down and licked at Niko's nipple again. Niko started panting almost immediately. He could feel Niko's cock hardening against him, taking an interest in what Vaska was doing.

"Niko," Vaska breathed quietly then leaned down to recapture Niko's lips. He felt Niko open up to him, and he swept his tongue inside to explore and conquer. The kiss seemed to go on forever. By the time Vaska lifted his head, he couldn't breathe. His heart pounded in his chest. Vaska stroked gentle patterns along Niko's jaw and neck. "My beautiful Niko."

"My mate," Niko replied, sending Vaska's world spinning out of control with two simple words.

Vaska inhaled softly. He suddenly couldn't get enough of the man. His hands moved over Niko's shoulders and chest, touching, caressing, and squeezing. Niko's hands answered in kind, sliding along the skin of Vaska's back and sides.

"On your hands and knees, majiktoka," Vaska said as he gently slapped Niko's hip. "I need to claim you again."

Vaska was surprised by the swiftness in Niko as the man rolled over and climbed to his hands and knees. Niko seemed as eager for them to be bonded as Vaska was. Vaska could only hope so. Claiming Niko was more important than breathing.

Vaska grabbed for the lube out of the nightstand drawer. He needed to be inside of his mate in the next five seconds or explode without him. He opened the small bottle of lube and squirted some out, generously lubing his cock then adding some between Niko's ass cheeks.

Vaska took his time stretching Niko out, drawing out the pleasure he knew Niko was experiencing. He wanted Niko to enjoy every moment of it, each finger, each thrust. He wasn't just claiming Niko as his mate, he was loving him with his body.

"Are you ready for me?"

His only response was a deep groan from Niko. He took it as a yes.

Vaska grabbed Niko's hips and pushed the head of his cock against the man's tight puckered hole, slowly pushing his way inside. Vaska groaned as he felt his cock become surrounded by soft, silken muscles.

Vaska began to move inside of Niko once his cock was completely buried, slowly at first, pulling almost completely out and then pushing it back in to the root. Little by little, his speed began to increase until he pounded into Niko's tight grip with a ferocity that surprised even Vaska.

Vaska could hear Niko panting and groaning beneath him. He needed his mate to feel the same pleasure that coursed through his own body. Vaska reached under Niko and grabbed the man's hard cock, stroking hard and fast. Within an instant, Vaska felt Niko's wet warmth splash over his fingers. Niko's ass clenched and quivered, squeezing Vaska in the most amazing manner.

Vaska leaned over Niko's back. Just as he felt himself start slipping over the edge into bliss, he buried his sharp canines into the soft skin between Niko's neck and shoulder. Vaska felt his balls tighten up and his cock swell. He released Niko's shoulder and tossed back his head, growling deep and low and needy as he erupted inside of his mate.

Still connected to Niko, Vaska rolled to his side, taking Niko with him. He wrapped his arms around Niko's chest and pulled the man's body back against his. A small shudder rocked Niko's body as Vaska licked at the mating bite on Niko's shoulder.

"Mine now, majiktoka," Vaska whispered against Niko's hot skin, "and I'm keeping you."

"Yes." Niko's words sounded sleepy and satisfied.

Vaska grinned. "That's yes, Your Imperial Highness."

"Not in this century." Niko chuckled then rolled just a bit until he could look over his shoulder at Vaska. "Seriously, though, how are you feeling? You were in pretty bad shape when we brought you up here yesterday."

"I feel fine." Vaska shrugged. "Which is a little odd considering what kind of shape I was in. I do remember being in a fight."

"You shifted right after Markus, Jonathan, and I brought you up here last night. Your wounds cleared right up after that."

"You met Jonathan?"

Niko nodded. "I met everyone last night. Well, except Antonio. He was hiding under a blanket and wouldn't come out."

"Yeah, he does that."

"What happened to him, Vaska?"

Vaska grimaced. "I don't rightly know. He doesn't talk much, and he refuses to talk about what happened to him. I'm not sure we'll ever know. It seems too painful for Antonio to talk about."

Vaska felt like he held heaven in his arms when Niko turned back around to face forward and cuddled back against him. He just couldn't seem to get past Niko's refusal in the beginning and needed to know why the man accepted him now.

"Niko, why now?"

"Why now what?"

"You've been so insistent that you didn't want to be mated. What changed your mind?"

"You did."

"Me?"

"You need a keeper."

Vaska blinked for several moments, stunned by Niko's words. "I need a keeper?"

Niko chuckled as he grabbed Vaska's hand in his and brought it to his mouth, planting a small kiss on the top. "You take too many chances with your life, and you have no one to back you up and keep you safe. I guess I finally realized that you needed me."

"I do need you, Niko, but—"

Niko turned and pressed a finger over Vaska's lips. "You need me, Vaska, whether you think so or not. And as much as I admire what you're trying to do here with the Tri Omegas, it has nothing to do with us. Your life and your safety do, however, and I'm not about to let anything happen to you."

Vaska grinned at the fierceness he could hear in Niko's voice. It was nice to know that someone had his back. He just hoped that the need Niko had to look after him grew into something more. He wanted Niko's heart as well as his protection.

He'd made it past the first hurdle. Niko accepted him and accepted their mating. The next hurdle would be making Niko want to be there because he wanted to and not because he felt he needed to protect him.

"So, what exactly happened last night?" Niko asked. "You passed out before you could tell me."

"Hunters attacked us."

"Hunters?" Niko frowned. "What in the hell is a hunter?"

"Wolf hunters, majiktoka."

Niko's eyebrows shot up. "Seriously?"

"You've never encountered a hunter before?" Vaska thought everyone knew of the wolf hunters. He had since he was a small child.

"No. Have you had much experience with them?"

"More often than I would like. Hunters have established groups all over the world, Niko. They are radicals, humans that know about us and believe that we are abominations to the world. They want to wipe us out."

Niko inhaled sharply and pushed away. Vaska groaned, partly in protest and partly at the sensation of Niko's tight grip moving over his cock as Niko pulled away, and he fell from the man's ass.

"Vaska," Niko said as he sat up, "the man that attacked me the other night, he kept calling me an abomination."

Vaska growled and clenched his hands against Niko. "He was trying to kill you."

"He almost succeeded."

"I followed you, trying to keep an eye on you." Vaska frowned and wrapped his arms tighter around Niko, pulling the man back down beside him. "I knew I shouldn't have left you. It wasn't safe, but I thought if you got back to your room, well—"

"Wait, you knew it wasn't safe?"

"I told you it wasn't, Niko. Remember?"

"Well, yeah but I thought…hell, I don't know what I thought, but I never imagined hunters would be after me."

"Us, they were after us, not just you. In fact, I'm not sure they were after you at all. I've had a price on my head for awhile now."

"They attacked me because of you?"

"More than likely." And that thought drove Vaska crazy. He should be able to protect his mate, not put him in the line of fire. Just by mating Niko, Vaska had put his life in danger. "You need to be extra conscious of your surroundings now, Niko. If the hunters discover that we're mated, and they will, your life will be in even more danger."

"Why?"

"You have to understand, Niko, there are two types of hunters. The first group are the ones that respect our right to live but will take us out if we become rogue. They feel that it is their duty to police us and keep us in line."

"And the second group?"

"They are far worse. They want us wiped off the face of the earth no matter what. They kill every werewolf they run across, man, woman, or child. They just don't care. It is their sole mission in life to kill all of us."

"But why? We've never done anything to them." Niko frowned. "Have we?"

"It happens from time to time. One of us goes rogue and attacks, killing humans. It doesn't show what most of us are like, but unfortunately, that's what they see. They believe that we are all the same, uncontrolled monsters that need to be eliminated."

"Is there any way to stop them?"

"I don't know. The less threatening hunters refuse to step in and stop the more radical ones. They feel that is not their place to interfere."

"Even though hunting us down might cause more problems?"

Vaska nodded. "If others take us out, they can let us die with a free conscience. They don't want to be responsible for our deaths unless we go rogue, but they won't stop someone else from killing us."

"That's just as bad."

"To us, yes. To them, it's a solution to their problem."

"That just doesn't make sense, Vaska."

"No, it doesn't, but it is what it is. Until they understand that a majority of us just want to live our lives in peace and quiet, we'll always have a problem with them. The number of us that go rogue is so small, but they have a far larger impact on how the hunters think than the rest of us. They truly see us as monsters."

"Maybe they should meet Ana or Uri, then they'd see that we're just like everyone else."

"I'm not sure Ana would be the best example." Vaska chuckled. "That girl has her own way of thinking about things, and she's not afraid to let everyone know about it."

"Well, Uri then. No one could look at that sweet little baby and think he's a monster."

"But that sweet little baby is going to grow up, Niko. And when he does, he will be able to shift and become what the hunters fear the most."

"An abomination?" Niko snorted.

"Someone faster and stronger than them, someone more powerful. I think that scares them the most, Niko. We're different than they are, and most people disdain anyone that is different."

"We're not that different, Vaska. We all basically want the same things, a safe place to live and raise our families."

"Yeah?" Vaska tilted his head and peered down at Niko. "Is that what you want?"

"I'm finding what I thought I wanted is a little different than it was three days ago, so I'll have to get back to you on that when I figure it out myself."

"I'll be waiting."

Niko laughed. "You do that, Your Imperial Highness."

"Yeah, you're having a little too much fun with that title of mine."

"I thought you were handing the title over to Uri?"

"I am, but someone has to hold onto it until he's old enough to carry it himself. It's a little big for him right now."

"Yeah." Niko laughed and wiggled his butt against Vaska's groin. "There's a lot of that happening around here."

"I didn't hear you complaining when I was balls deep in your ass."

"Who was complaining? I was just stating a fact."

Vaska growled and started to roll over on top of Niko when a feral, pain-filled cry echoed through the room. Vaska froze, his muscles tensing as he covered Niko with his body. He glanced wildly around the room looking for whatever threat might be coming their way.

"What the hell was that?" Niko asked.

As the loud cry filled the room again, Vaska suddenly remembered the hunter he faced the previous night. The fight between them had been brutal, the hunter fighting with a fierceness that surprised Vaska. Vaska almost thought he might lose.

With the fear of what would happen to Niko spurring him on, Vaska had eventually overpowered the hunter. He'd tied the man up and locked him in a hidden cell in the secret passageway, as far away from Niko as he could be.

"I think it's our guest."

"Our what?"

Vaska rolled to the side of the bed and climbed off the bed. He went right over to his dresser and pulled out some clean jeans then pulled them on. He tossed a clean shirt at Niko and grabbed one for himself.

"Get dressed and I'll introduce you."

"To who?"

"The perimeter alarm was set off last night by a hunter. Somehow he made it inside the house before I found him. He also discovered the secret passageway into the pantry. We fought, and I was able to subdue him, but I couldn't let him escape, not with the knowledge he had. There's no telling what he would do with it."

"Damn, Vaska," Niko said as he climbed from bed and quickly got dressed, "we need to get those people out of there and somewhere safe."

"Where, Niko? These people need to be safe from the hunters and from packs that want them for their power. Can you think of a single place they would be safe from both?"

"Yes, actually I can."

Vaska frowned then crossed his arms over his chest. "I'm listening."

"Have you ever heard of a place called Vourdala Island?"

"Isn't that where you're from?"

"It is." Niko nodded. "Vourdala Island is totally self-contained. It can only be reached by sea and ferry boat. It's also governed by a man I trust with my life, my brother, Vadim."

"Your alpha."

"Yes. Vadim understands about Tri Omegas. He's friends with several and even has one living in his house, a man named Ryland."

"Viktor Stylianos's mate?"

"Right again. Viktor and his two mates, Ryland and Gregory, live in the alpha Compound with Vadim and Sasha. I have every belief that if we get your Tri Omegas to Vourdala Island, Vadim will not only welcome them, he will do everything within his power to keep them safe."

"Don't you think we should ask him first instead of just showing up?"

"Vadim and Sasha are on their way here, remember?" Niko chuckled. "We can ask him then, but I know he'll do the right thing. Vadim always does, especially when it comes to Sasha's safety."

"Sasha? What does he have to do with this?"

"If what you say is true and these hunters are after us, then Sasha is in danger."

"And?" Vaska was confused. He didn't understand what Sasha's safety had to do with Vadim agreeing to accept the Tri Omegas on his island.

"Vadim will do everything in his power to keep Sasha safe, even if that means taking on a bunch of Tri Omegas and one Grand Prince. Hell, he'd take on the devil himself if it meant keeping Sasha safe."

"You might want to add one human hunter into that, Niko. Until we get a chance to figure this guy out I don't know if it's safe to let him free. He seemed to know right where the secret passage to the basement was and went right for it. I don't know how much he knows."

"I get it. I still think moving everyone to Vourdala Island is our best bet. We can better protect them there. It would also give them a chance at a semi-normal life. No one in Vadim's pack will treat them any differently because they are Tri Omegas."

"You might be right, but we'll have to discuss it with everyone first, including those downstairs. I won't make decisions about their lives without their say so. It wouldn't be right, Niko."

"No, I understand, and I think it's commendable of you to take their wants and needs into account. That shows what kind of man you are."

Vaska glanced down at the floor when he felt his face flush slightly. "Yeah, well, remember you said that when you meet this hunter. I can't promise that I won't have to kill him if he proves to be a danger to you, me, or the others."

Niko patted Vaska's chest. "Let's go see what's up with him before we decide anything. We might be able to talk some sense into him."

"Seriously doubtful, majiktoka, but I applaud your optimism."

Vaska crossed back to the fireplace passage and hit the secret release buttons. The little door at the back of the fireplace swung open, and he climbed through, Niko fast on his heels.

"Just where do you have this guy?"

"There's some hidden cells down the passageway," Vaska said as he led the way. "I think they were originally set up to hold rogue wolves, but since this house was passed to me when my father died, I can't be sure."

"This wasn't your brother's house?"

"No. The estate my brother inherited along with the family title is closer to town. This is considered the country estate."

"Country estate?" Niko whistled. "Damn! I mated into money."

Vaska always worried that his title would mean more to his mate than he did. Niko's words didn't help any. He didn't want Niko to think he was made of luxury and that their life would be spent living the high life. It wouldn't, not by any means.

"Don't let the estate and title fool you, Niko. All of my money has gone into helping the Tri Omegas and keeping things running. I'm dirt-ass poor."

Niko snorted. "Oh please, like I'm interested in anything but your gorgeous ass. I could care less about your money or title."

Vaska preened a little at Niko's words as he turned in the narrow passage to look back at him. "You think my ass is gorgeous?"

"I'd like it even more if you'd let me fuck it."

Vaska almost stumbled in shock. "You want to fuck me?"

"Duh."

Chapter 8

Niko chuckled at the shocked look on Vaska's face. He truly seemed stunned by the fact that Niko wanted to fuck him. Niko couldn't understand why. Vaska was gorgeous. He'd have to be dead for six months not to be interested in fucking Vaska, and even then it was iffy.

"Of course I want to fuck you. Do I look stupid to you?"

"No, I guess I just never thought of it."

Those words gave Niko pause. He clenched his hands to keep from growling. "Do I look like that much of a bottom boy to you?"

"No." Vaska snorted. "I'm that much of a top. I've never bottomed in my life."

Those words disappointed Niko, but he knew he couldn't expect anything less. Vaska shouted dominant from the top of his head to the tip of his toes. No one would ever picture him as a bottom. He was too intimidating.

It wasn't that Niko thought being on the bottom made him any less masculine. It just put control of the situation, and the sex, firmly in Vaska's hands. Niko bemoaned the fact that he might never get to fuck Vaska. He could think of very little else he'd rather do.

"Maybe it's something you could think about?" Niko hedged.

Vaska didn't say anything for a moment. He seemed to be pondering the idea. Niko was just about to give up hope and tell Vaska to forget it when the man suddenly nodded.

"It's something that we would have to work up to, but I'm willing to try."

"Really?" Niko was a little shocked. He hoped Vaska would consider it. He just never actually thought he would.

"If we're going to be equal partners, then it's not fair that you always bottom for me. Our mating needs to be on equal footing, don't you think?"

Niko nodded eagerly. Trying was good enough for him. "I'm good with that."

Vaska started to grin then jerked when another howl filled the passageway. "Come on, we'd better go check on him. He's not sounding so good."

"He's sounds like a wolf, Vaska."

"Don't be ridiculous, Niko. He's a hunter. He wants to kill us, not be one of us. He's probably trying to get our attention."

Niko rolled his eyes at the patronizing tone in Vaska's voice. Sometimes the man could be too much of an alpha male. It reminded Niko of his brother, Vadim. "I still think he sounds like a wolf."

Vaska didn't say anything, just stopped in front of a thick steel door. Niko could hear noises from inside, soft cries of pain. He frowned at Vaska. "What did you do to him?"

"Subdued him and tied him up."

"He sounds like he's dying."

"He's obviously trying to trick us, Niko. At the first opportunity he'll try and escape or kill us both." Vaska pointed a finger at Niko. "I've dealt with this type before, Niko. Don't underestimate him just because you think he's in pain."

Niko nodded. He had to take Vaska's word on it. He had never met a hunter as far as he knew. If Vaska said the guy was dangerous, Niko believed him. Still, the man inside the small cell sounded like he was in a lot of pain.

Vaska cautiously opened the door then stepped inside. Niko walked in behind him, his eyes quickly scanning the cold stone cell until they fell on the figure of a man curled up in the corner of the room.

"Well, there he is," Vaska said, waving a hand at the man, "the great wolf hunter."

"Vaska!"

Niko kept his eyes firmly on the man as he slowly walked closer. At the first sign of movement, he wanted to be ready to defend himself. The closer he got, the more Niko could see the small shivers rocking the man's curled body. He seemed about ready to shake apart.

"Are you sure he wasn't severely injured, Vaska?"

"Well." Vaska didn't sound so sure. "He didn't look horribly injured, if that's what you mean. He had a few scrapes and scratches, but there were no deep wounds."

The man didn't move when Niko reached him and knelt down beside him. Niko didn't know whether to be concerned or scared. Was he just play acting, waiting for Niko to get close enough to attack, or was he really injured?

Niko glanced over his shoulder at Vaska, nodding to the spot just at the top of the man's prone form. Once Vaska walked over, Niko reached down and grabbed the man by the arms, slowly turning him onto his back.

"Vaska, wha—" Niko stopped talking as shock overrode his ability to speak.

The man he stared down at didn't look like the lethal hunter Vaska had described. Niko wasn't sure exactly what he expected, but it wasn't the sunken eyes and prominent cheekbones. The color around the man's eyes was all grayish blue, his skin pale. He looked almost fragile.

"This is your hunter?" Niko whispered as he looked up at Vaska in horror.

"Niko, this isn't—" Vaska looked almost as horrified as Niko felt. "I don't know what's going on here, but he didn't look like this when I left him in here. Maybe he took poison or something."

Niko quickly checked the man's lips. Besides looking incredibly pale, there seemed to be no signs that the man had ingested anything he shouldn't have. Of course, he could have and not shown any outward signs.

"Let's get him back into the bedroom where we can clean him up and check him over. He may be a hunter, but I'm not sure I want his death on our hands, not when he obviously can't defend himself."

"Niko, I'm not sure that's a good idea."

"Vaska, I'm not going to let this man die, not on our watch." Niko reached down to get his arms under the man's body. He grunted when his strength wasn't enough to lift the hunter. "Help me?"

Vaska let out a loud sigh then leaned down to lift the man's upper body into his arms. Niko grabbed the man's legs. Together, they lifted the man into the air and started carrying him out of the small stone cell and down the hallway.

"If it makes you feel better, we can tie him down to the bed after we strip his clothes off."

"It would."

Niko smirked. His mate was so protective, almost overly so. Niko guessed Vaska had a right to be. He'd been dealing with the hunters far longer than Niko. Vaska had a right to his paranoia.

"Let's lay him down on the bed," Niko said as they entered the bedroom again. "You can tie him down while I get something to clean him up."

"What about his clothes?" Vaska asked as they laid the large man down on the bed.

"We'll cut them off."

Vaska smiled as if he found the idea amusing. Niko rolled his eyes and walked into the bathroom to get something to clean the man up. He found a small bowl under the sink and filled it with hot water. He also found a small first aid kit, a couple of washcloths, and a towel.

Grabbing everything, Niko carried them all back into the bedroom. Vaska was just getting done tying the man down to the bed when he walked back into the room. Niko set everything down on the nightstand then stood beside the bed.

It was only as the bedroom lights fell on the man that Niko felt a niggle of recognition. "Vaska, I think this is the guy that attacked me the other night." The sunlight-blond hair looked very familiar. If the man had milky blue eyes, Niko knew he would be right.

"This guy?"

Niko nodded. "I could be wrong. I didn't get that good of a look at the guy that attacked me. But I'm pretty sure. That blond hair is kind of hard to miss."

"Well, it would make sense if he was. While there are hunters all over the world, there aren't that many in any one place. They tend to stay in small groups or work alone."

"Could he be working with someone then?" Niko glanced over at the window as a small thread of panic started to take root. "Could more hunters be out there waiting to attack us?"

"That's always a possibility, Niko."

Niko shook his head. "We really need to get home, Vaska. We would be safe there. Everyone would be safe there. No one is allowed on the island unless they've passed through our security, not even members of the council."

"Seriously?" Vaska's eyebrows shot up. "You make the Wolf Council go through security?"

"Of course. Vadim doesn't let anyone on the island that might be a threat to our pack or Sasha."

"Wow, that man really takes his protection of his mate seriously."

"You have no idea." Niko chuckled. "Just wait until you meet Sasha and you'll understand. While he is cute and adorable in his own way, the man is a complete klutz. He trips over air. He also thinks it's his mission in life to bring"—Niko made quotation marks in the air with his fingers—"peace and joy into Vadim's life."

"That doesn't sound so bad"

"It wouldn't be if Sasha thought ahead. Unfortunately, he comes up with these great ideas then loses his fucking mind. He once planned a romantic candlelight picnic for Vadim and almost burned down the entire forest when he tied taper candles to the tree branches. It took us most of the night to put out the fire."

Niko laughed when Vaska just blinked at him. "He means well, he really does. He just tends to not think ahead."

"Is he dangerous?"

"Only to Vadim." Niko snickered then sobered and held up a hand. "Don't get me wrong. Sasha can be a trip, but he'd gladly give up his life for Vadim. And don't let his small size fool you. He once took out two wolves when they attacked Vadim. Even shot with a bullet, he still tried to keep Vadim safe. His entire world is Vadim, well, Vadim and their kids."

"Kids?"

Niko nodded. "Vadim and Sasha have three kids. Ivan, Marika, Riana. Marika was the son of a very dear friend of Vadim's. When his parents were killed, Vadim took Marika in. Ivan is Vadim's biological son and Riana is Sasha's biological daughter."

"What about their mothers?"

"Ivan's mother died, and Riana's mother still lives on the island. She was a surrogate arranged by Vadim and Sasha. Last time I heard, she was getting ready to get married and move to her future husband's pack."

"And she doesn't mind leaving her child behind?"

Niko shrugged. "Sasha says not everyone is made to be a parent. Karina loves Riana, but she realizes she's not parenting material. She seems happy to let Sasha raise Riana and come visit when she can."

"I'm not sure I could ever give up a child of mine."

"I don't either, but I agree with Sasha. Not everyone is cut out to be a parent. It doesn't mean that Karina loves Riana any less. It just means that she's not able to be a fulltime parent. I actually think it's commendable of her to know that and allow Sasha to have Riana fulltime. Sasha is a wonderful parent."

"How do you feel about children?"

Niko almost swallowed his tongue. "I think I need to get used to being mated before we even begin to discuss children."

Vaska chuckled.

"One thing at a time, Vaska." Niko glanced back at the man on the bed. "For right now, let's deal with this. We need to find out how injured this guy is before we do anything else."

"Agreed."

"How exactly do you want to do this?" Niko didn't have a clue.

"Well, did you bring a towel with you?"

Niko nodded and reached over to the nightstand to grab one.

"While I pull his pants off, why don't you cover his bits and pieces? No sense freaking the guy out more than we need to."

"And you don't think he's going to freak when he wakes up and finds himself tied down to your bed with two wolves standing over him?" Niko would flip if he was in the same position.

Vaska chuckled. "Yeah, I can see that. That doesn't mean I'm going to untie him anytime soon."

"No, I get that." Niko grabbed the towel and spread it over the man's waist, taking note of the nipple ring the man had that sported a red, shiny gem. Interesting. "So, let's do this then."

"Unbutton his pants," Vaska said as he walked to the bottom of the bed and pulled the man's boots off then grabbed the hem of his pants.

Niko did as Vaska directed then watched him yank the man's pants down. Niko almost lifted the towel to look at the guy's bits and pieces but thought better of it when Vaska growled at him.

"Sorry, old habits die hard."

"Just as long as they die, Niko."

"Yeah, yeah." Niko chuckled. "Let's get this shirt off of him."

Vaska came around to the other side of the bed and together they got the man's shirt off of him. As pale and gaunt as the man was, he was still a very big man. By the time Niko and Vaska had him naked, they were both breathing heavily, and it wasn't the fun kind of heavy breathing either.

"Was he this skinny when he attacked you, Niko?" Vaska asked. "He doesn't look like he could hurt a fly let alone a wolf."

"I didn't really take the time look, Vaska. I was too busy getting my ass whooped."

"By him?" Vaska pointed, frowning.

"Yes, by him, and don't look so surprised. He did a number on you too, remember?"

"It just doesn't seem possible."

Niko had to agree. The man lying before them didn't look like he could do much of anything without assistance. He was tall. His feet hung off the bottom of the bed. But he was also pretty much skin and bones.

"I don't get it, Vaska. How could this man beat the both of us like he did? I might understand it if he were a shifter, but he's human."

"Let's figure that out later. Right now, we need to make sure he wasn't hurt too badly. It might not explain why he looks the way he does, but at least I'd feel a little better."

Niko nodded. He reached over and dipped two of the washcloths into the hot water then rung them out. After handing one to Vaska, Niko began washing the dirt, grime, and blood off the unconscious man.

While the face and body he revealed was breathtaking in its own way, it was still pale white and gaunt. The man's hips were bony and protruding, almost as if the man hadn't eaten in days.

"He must have been starving, Vaska. No wonder he attacked us. He was probably trying to mug us."

"Yeah maybe, but it still doesn't explain how he knew about the secret passage."

"Maybe he was just trying to get to the food in the pantry?"

Vaska frowned. "Maybe."

"Why don't you go have Markus prepare him something to eat, something not heavy, like soup or porridge. I'll check him over for injuries." Niko noted several small cuts and abrasions on the man as well as a couple of bite marks. He pointed to the one on the man's chest. "I think that one is mine."

Vaska smirked and pointed to the one on the man's neck. "That one is definitely mine."

"So, we both bit him?"

"Looks that way."

"Good thing we can't pass on the wolf gene or this guy would be fucked." Niko chuckled as he finished wiping the man off. Once he was assured he could see all of the injuries on him, Niko grabbed some antiseptic and started cleaning each wound, one by one.

Niko was leaning close to the man's throat, cleaning the bite marks Vaska left on his skin, when his vision suddenly went black and white as his eyes turned lupine, his canines dropped down, and his cock hardened until it hurt. He inhaled sharply, more of the man's heavenly scent filling him, and glanced up Vaska.

"I think we have a problem, Vaska."

"What?"

Niko sat up and gestured to the unconscious man. "Sniff him."

"What?" Vaska snapped. He had his hands on his hips. His eyes were narrowed to little slits. He looked outraged.

"Please?"

Vaska rolled his eyes and leaned down to sniff at the man's neck. Niko knew he was right in his suspicions when Vaska's body suddenly stiffened. His face turned pasty white as he glanced up at Niko.

"What the hell is going on, Niko?" Vaska whispered. "He smells like mate."

Niko shook his head and looked back down at the man between them. A shiver of fear and foreboding shook his body. "I know."

"How is that possible? He's human." Vaska stood up and started pacing beside the bed. He wrung his hands together for a moment then pushed them through his thick black hair. He kept looking back down at the unconscious man.

"Is he?"

"He has to be." Vaska stopped pacing and stared. "Right?"

"I'm beginning to wonder, Vaska. I mean, nothing says we couldn't end up mated to a human, I suppose, but what are the odds?" Niko glanced down at the sunlight-blond-haired man. "Is there any way he could be one of us?"

Chapter 9

Serge could hear muted voices talking above him. He knew he wasn't alone in the room. He just couldn't quite make out what the people talking were saying. Their voices were jumbled, faint.

Serge tried to hide his confusion by pretending to be asleep. He didn't know where he was, and he didn't know who was talking. In his line of work, that meant danger. He could only hope they would leave soon and give him a chance to escape.

The throbbing in his head said that it might take awhile before the words being spoken over him made sense. Serge wasn't sure why his head hurt. Although he remembered a fight, Serge didn't remember getting hit in the head. He was pretty sure he'd fought the good fight.

"…one of us?"

That perked Serge's interest. He was starting to understand what the two men above him were saying. At least, they sounded like men. Their voices were deep, masculine. Serge assumed they were men. Of course, he'd been wrong before. There were some women out there with some pretty deep voices.

"There's always a chance, Niko," someone else said. "I just don't see how it could have happened. He's a hunter."

Serge prayed that the sudden stillness in his body wasn't noticed by the two men. He could feel his heart pounding furiously in his chest, almost to the point of being painful. It matched the pain in the rest of his body.

"We're never going to find out until he wakes up and we can talk to him."

And not even then if Serge had anything to do with it. The first opportunity he got, he was gone. Serge didn't know who these men were, but he didn't like the vibes he got from them. He felt like his very skin ached just from hearing them speak. It wasn't a comfortable feeling.

"So, what do you want me to do about it, Niko? It's not like I can revive him. And look at him. It's doubtful he's going to be able to tell us anything until he heals."

"Then we need to make sure he does heal, because we need some answers, Vaska. I want to know who he is and why he smells the way he does. Only you are supposed to smell that way."

Both men sounded disturbed, upset. Serge didn't know how that boded for him. It was obvious from their words that the two men knew he was a hunter. It was also obvious that Serge was injured in some manner. The aches and pains in his body attested to that.

Serge assumed he got them in the fight, but he couldn't be sure. He remembered enough to know he had gone out to the Federov estate after receiving information about a secret ritual happening where humans were being sacrificed to their heathen's gods. He was determined to make sure that didn't happen.

After receiving his information from an anonymous source, Serge had snuck into the estate. It hadn't been hard. No one was patrolling the property lines. He was amazed at how easy it had been, actually. A quick run through the massive grounds and little finagling with the backdoor to the kitchen and he'd gained access.

His informant had given him clear directions to a hidden cavern underneath the estate. He mentioned the pantry, the hidden entrance in the pantry, and even which stones to touch to get the pantry entrance to open. He was spot on.

Serge thought he'd been successful in gaining entrance until he ran smack dab into Vasiliy Federov. He'd know the man anywhere. Serge had been hunting him for nearly a year. The Grand Prince of the wolves had a huge price on his head, one that Serge had every intention of collecting.

Unfortunately, Serge didn't remember anything that had happened after the fight started. The rest was all a blur. Serge either lost the fight and was now a prisoner of the wolves, or he had escaped and someone was caring for him. He wouldn't know until he opened his eyes, but once he did, they would know he was awake.

Serge decided on a different route and groaned loudly. Maybe he could convince whoever had him that he didn't remember a thing. If they thought he had some memory loss and they let their guard down, he could escape.

At least it was a plan.

"Can you hear me?"

Serge groaned again. He felt a wet cloth wipe across his forehead. A rough callused hand brushed the hair back from his cheeks. Whoever had him seemed to have a gentle touch. Serge wondered if that would continue.

Serge moaned and fluttered his eyes. Once they started to open, he didn't need to pretend to flutter them. The bright lights in the room made his eyeballs ache. When he finally got them open all of the way, Serge inhaled sharply.

Two of the most gorgeous men he'd ever seen in his life leaned over him. One of them Serge recognized as Vasiliy Federov, and that sent a shiver of dread racing through him. The other one Serge didn't know, but he wished he did. He was just as breathtaking as Vasiliy.

"Hey, how are you feeling?" the stranger asked.

Serge frowned. "Where am I?"

The man glanced at the other man for a moment then back down at him. "You're at the Federov estate but you're safe."

"What happened?"

"Uh, you were in a fight."

"A fight?" Of course he was in a fucking fight. He already knew that, and he knew exactly who he fought with, Vasiliy Federov, the man standing on the other side of him. Although, he was curious how they would explain the injuries he could feel on his body. "What fight?"

"You don't remember?"

Serge shook his head then gave a real groan when shards of pain splintered through his head. He tried to reach up and grab his head only to find his hands restrained. Serge's eyes widened as he looked first at one hand then the other. He started jerking his arms, trying to escape his bonds.

"Why am I tied up?"

"It's for your own good," Vaska said. "Calm down."

"Calm down?" Serge snapped. "I don't want to calm down. I want to know why in the hell I'm tied up."

The men glanced at each other for several moments. Serge didn't know what they saw in each other's expressions, but when they looked back, Vaska leaned over and untied his hands. Serge waited until his hands were free then quickly scooted up to the top of the bed and sat up. He rubbed his wrists as he eyed both men.

"Why was I tied up?"

"Because you tried to kill me," Vaska said.

"I what?" *Duh!* Vaska was a wolf shifter. Of course Serge tried to kill him. He'd made it his mission in life to kill every wolf he could find. They didn't deserve to live. They were monsters.

"You...tried...to...kill...me," Vaska said slowly.

Serge blinked. Okay, now the man was just being an asshole. Serge wasn't stupid, not by a long shot. Vaska was talking to him like he didn't have two brain cells to rub together. Still, Serge had to play stupid, as much as it grated on his nerves.

"Why would I try to kill you?"

"Gee, I don't know," Vaska said sarcastically. He crossed his arms over his chest and glared. "Because you're a—"

"Vaska!" the other man snapped as he jumped to his feet and walked around the bed to stand next to Vaska. "Now is not the time."

"Now is the perfect time, Niko."

"Let's get him fed and rested first." Serge watched Niko's hand land on Vaska's arm, stroking his skin. "We can question him when he's all healed up."

"Niko, even injured he's dangerous. He'll slit your throat the first chance he gets."

Serge almost smirked. He'd slit Vaska's throat the first chance he got and dance in his blood. If the other man, Niko, turned out to be a wolf as well, and Serge was beginning to think he was, he'd do the same to him.

He was bound and determined to kill every wolf he could find until not a single one of them was left alive on the planet. Serge hated wolves with every fiber of his being. They destroyed his life, and he was going to make each and every one of them pay.

"Why do you hate me so much?" Serge asked. "What have I ever done to you?"

Vaska's gaze was intense when he turned to look at Serge, his deep blue eyes filled with distain. "You tried to kill my mate."

"Your mate?"

"Me," the other man answered.

"You?" Serge racked his brain and tried to remember if he had ever fought the brown-haired man standing beside the bed. He suddenly remembered the fight he'd had with an unknown assailant a few nights previous.

He'd been following Vaska and a friend when he saw them kiss. He knew they were involved in some manner. When the two men separated, Serge had followed the stranger, curious as to why he was involved with a wolf. He just meant to scare the man, to get him to stop hanging out with Vaska. He wanted Vaska to be miserable before he killed the guy.

But the stranger had fought back, stabbing his razor-sharp claws into Serge's thigh. Serge had known instantly that the man he fought with was a wolf. He tried to kill the stranger, but the man put up too much of a fight. He injured Serge to the point where he knew retreating was his only choice. He still had claw and teeth marks.

Serge still spent a day in bed from his injuries. He probably should have spent more time healing, but an anonymous phone call had sent him to the Federov estate instead. It was beginning to look like he might have been set up, though.

"That was you?" Serge asked then suddenly realized what he had given away when both men stared down at him.

"Yes, that was me," the brown-haired man said, holding out his hand. "Nikolai Miroslav, nice to meet you."

Serge stared at the man's hand for the longest time, not sure if he should shake it or not. He had heard of Nikolai Miroslav, the Beta of the Vourdala Pack. The man had a reputation for being a player in the wolf world and a killer in the human world. Serge wished he'd killed him when he had the chance.

He folded his arms across his chest, refusing to shake the man's hand. Nikolai Miroslav might want to play nice. Serge did not. Vaska was right. He'd slit the wolf's throat the first chance he got.

"Well, I can see your mother didn't raise you with any manners," Niko said as he dropped his hand back to his side.

"My mother is dead. She was killed by wolves, as was my father and brother." Serge arched an eyebrow at the surprised looks on the faces of the two men. "Just as I will kill you."

"I am truly sorry to hear of the death of your family," Niko said. "However, I did not kill them. I would appreciate it if you stopped trying to kill me."

"Are you for real?" Serge scoffed.

"I believe I am," Niko said. "I have never harmed you or yours. I see no reason for you to hold me to blame for something I did not do."

"You're a wolf!"

"I'm fully aware of that fact." Niko smiled. "I've been a wolf all of my life."

"You're an abomination."

Niko rolled his eyes. "Oh please, you can't come up with something better than that?"

"How man humans have you killed?"

"How many wolves have you killed?" Niko countered.

"As many as I can."

"Ah see, that's where we're different. I only kill in defense of myself or my pack. I don't kill because I hate someone." Niko tapped his fingers together. "Somehow I think that makes you the abomination."

Serge growled low in his throat and dove off the bed, trying to get to Niko. His hands curled into fists. He aimed them at Niko's neck, wishing he had a knife instead. Just as he reached Niko, he was slammed back onto the bed so fast the air was driven from his lungs.

Serge jerked and cried out as sharp canine teeth sank into his throat. His vision blurred as blood was sucked from the wound in his neck. He clutched desperately at the body holding him down, his heart thundering. He was going to die, and he knew it.

"Vaska, that's enough. Let him go before you hurt him."

Serge was shocked when the teeth in his neck were slowly pulled free. He felt Vaska's tongue lick across the bite mark and shivered. His greatest shame was the slight arousal he felt when the man's tongue stroked his flesh and the disappointment that nearly shattered him when Vaska stopped.

Serge couldn't look at the man when Vaska stood up. He wondered if either man could read the humiliation on his face. He looked up at Vaska through his eyelashes, then Niko. Both men were breathing heavily, Vaska more than Niko.

There seemed to be some sort of silent communication going on between them as they looked at each other. Serge just wondered what it was. Had they noticed the reactions in Serge's body to the feeling of Vaska's teeth in his throat? Did they see his embarrassment?

Would they use it against him?

"Let me go," Serge growled, deciding to take the road of indignant anger instead of letting either man know how much their mere presence affected him. "You can't hold me like this."

"I can do any damn thing I want to do," Vaska said. "You're on my land and that means you do what I say. I am the law here."

"Like I give a fuck." Serge snorted. "I wouldn't listen to you if you were the last man on earth."

"You will."

"Like hell I will."

"Where do you think you are?" Niko asked as he stepped forward and waved his hands around the room. "You're in the middle of wolf central, honey. You'd better get used to doing what you're told if you expect to live through the night."

"So kill me then!" Serge snapped. "Isn't that what you do? Kill people?"

"Not normally, no." Niko chuckled. "But I might be willing to make an exception for you."

Serge had no doubt from the intent glare in Niko's eyes that the man would do exactly what he said he would. Serge would have to bide his time until he could escape, but he wouldn't leave before he killed them both. Vasiliy Federov and Nikolai Miroslav both just moved to the top of his hit list.

"Fine."

Niko simply arched an eyebrow at him. Under normal circumstances, Serge would have found it attractive. But this wasn't normal circumstances. He was being held prisoner by a pack of wolves. He just glared back.

"Niko, go ask Markus to make us all something to eat. I'm sure Serge could use some food. His color looks a little better, but he needs real food to heal."

Serge turned to look at Vaska in shock. The big bad wolf was ordering him food so he could heal? Serge couldn't have been more surprised if the man had told him he was about to sprout wings and fly.

He opened his mouth to protest then thought better of it. If he hoped to have any chance of surviving until he could escape, he needed all of his strength. He also had a few cuts and abrasions, not to mention teeth marks, that needed to heal. Food and rest would go a long ways toward making that happen.

The moment Niko left the room, Vaska walked to the bottom of the bed. He glared down at Serge. "I want to make this perfectly clear to you. My mate has never dealt with one of your kind before. He doesn't know what kind of monster you can be."

"Monster?" Serge scoffed. "You call me a monster?"

"Yes, I do. You kill indiscriminately. Your kind kills men, women, and children. We kill for food and to defend ourselves from humans like you," Vaska sneered. "You don't even have the decency to let children live."

"Because they grow into wolves."

Serge hadn't personally ever killed a child, and he doubted he ever would. But he had heard of other hunters that did. He made sure he had only the top wolves on his extermination list just to prevent such a thing. It gave him the creeps.

"Yes, they do, but most of them have more compassion than I do. I would have killed you outright, but my mate has a softer heart than me. Touch a hair on his head again and I will forget what a nice guy I am."

"Do you really expect me to be scared of you?"

"Not at all." Vaska shook his head. "I'm not trying to scare you. I'm trying to warn you."

"Why? Why do you even care? Why not just kill me and get it over with?"

"Because that is not the way we work."

Serge gave Vaska a scathing look. "You expect me to believe that?"

"No."

Serge was confused by the sudden sadness he could see in Vaska's eyes. He was even more mystified by why it bothered him. Maybe he received a bump on the head. It could be the only explanation.

"No, I don't expect you to believe anything I say. You have far too much hate inside of you, especially for those that you do not understand. It's just too bad you never took the time to try and get to know the people you have been trying to wipe off the face of the earth."

"Get to know you?" Serge was stunned at Vaska's words. "Why in the hell would I want to get to know you? You're a monster."

Vaska sighed. "Yes, I imagine to you I am."

Vasiliy Federov confused the hell out of Serge. He'd heard a lot from other hunters about the man. He was in the top ten of most wanted wolves, hunted by every known wolf hunter for the price on his head and the right to say that they killed one of the most dangerous wolves alive.

Serge had a hard time equating the man before him with the monster he knew Vasiliy Federov to be. He didn't look like a monster by any means, but Serge knew this wasn't his true form either.

His body was just a bit smaller than Serge's, but his black hair and deep blue eyes were a dark contrast to Serge's sunlight-blond hair and milky blue eyes. If he'd simply been a man, Serge knew he could have taken Vaska. But he wasn't, and that was the problem.

Serge had sworn on his mother's grave to kill every wolf he could find. He'd spent the better part of his life training to be a hunter. The last year had been spent pursuing those that he felt were the worst of the worst, including Vasiliy Federov.

Coming face to face with the man made Serge feel a little uneasy. It wasn't that he had a problem killing a man he had spoken to or met in person. He just couldn't equate Vaska to the monster he knew

Vasiliy Federov to be. They seemed like two completely different people.

Serge jumped when the door opened and Niko walked back in carrying something in one arm, holding the hand of a small child in the other.

"Niko, what are you doing?" Vaska asked as he raced over to the man.

"Markus is making us something to eat, and Juliette is sleeping. He asked me to keep an eye on Ana and Uri for a few minutes. I thought Serge might want to meet them."

"Are you out of your mind?" Vaska growled. "He'll kill them the first chance he gets."

"I don't kill children!" Serge snapped.

"Don't you?" Vaska said vehemently as he whipped around. "Your kind wants all of us dead, don't they?"

Vaska turned around and grabbed the small bundle in Niko's arms and cradled it to his chest. He walked over and set it down in Serge's lap. "Here, go ahead. Kill him. He's just going to grow up and turn into a wolf. Why not take him out before he can become a danger to humans?"

Serge stared down at the small bundle on his lap with a bit of horror and a bit of curiosity. He gingerly reached down and pulled the edge of the fuzzy blue blanket back, revealing the small button-nosed chubby face of a newborn infant.

Serge swallowed hard. "He's a wolf?"

"Yes," Vaska replied. "Better yet, he's my nephew. That should give you an even bigger incentive to kill him."

Serge clenched his jaw as he glared up at Vaska. "I don't kill children," he growled through clenched teeth. "I've never killed a child in my life, and I won't start with him, even if he is your nephew."

"A hunter with ethics?" Vaska scoffed. "Will wonders never cease?"

"Vaska, be nice," Niko admonished with a small laugh before looking down at the small child beside him. "Ana, would you like to meet...uh..." Niko glanced up, frowning.

"Serge Dmitriev."

Niko smiled. "Ana, I'd like you to meet Serge Dmitriev. He's going to be a guest here for a few days."

The little girl let go of Niko's hand and waved, her chestnut curls bouncing around her head. She never pulled her thumb from her mouth. Just clutched a small blue blanket to her chest and stared at Serge. He found it a little unnerving, like she could read all of his secrets.

"Ana." Serge nodded at her.

"Ana's parents were killed, so she and her brother came to live here with Vaska."

Serge's eyes widened. "By hunters?"

"No, her parents were killed by the alpha of her pack."

"Oh?" Serge arched an eyebrow. He knew that the wolf packs weren't the nice peaceful people Vaska was trying to make them out to be. Niko just proved his point. He arched an eyebrow at Vaska. "Imagine that."

"I never said we weren't bloodthirsty, Serge," Vaska said as he reached down and lifted the baby out of Serge's lap and cradled him to his chest. "We have our moments just like everyone else. We also have our bad seeds like everyone else. However, not all of us are bad. Some of us just want to live in peace."

"You really expect me to believe that?" Serge clenched his fists then quickly pushed them under the edge of the blanket when Ana stared at them. For some reason he couldn't understand, Serge didn't want to scare the little girl. "I've seen what you can do with my own eyes. I know how dangerous you are."

"Oh, we're very dangerous, Serge." Vaska chuckled. "We protect what is ours at all costs. But we do not go out looking for trouble. That would be you humans."

"I only hunt because of what your kind did to my family. You killed all of them, my mother, my father, and even my brother, a mere child. You brought this on yourself."

"Me?" Vaska asked. "When did I kill your family?"

Serge growled, feeling exasperated with the big wolf. "You know what I mean."

"No." Vaska shook his head. "No, I don't, Serge. Tell me."

"Wolves killed my family."

"No."

Serge blinked and stared at Ana, watching her stick her thumb back into her mouth. It was the only word she said since entering the room, and spoken at almost a whisper, but it echoed around the room as if she shouted it.

"What do you mean, Ana?" Niko asked as he squatted down in front of her.

Ana pulled her thumb from her mouth, staring across at Serge with such intensity that he began to fidget under her gaze. "We didn't kill Serge's family. Human hunters did, the same ones that taught him to be a hunter."

"Why would they do that, Ana?" Niko asked.

Yeah, why? Serge wondered.

Ana stared at all of them as if to say *well, duh*. "Cause he's one of us."

"One of us?"

"Serge is a wolf."

Chapter 10

Vaska could see the storm that was brewing in the tensing of Serge's muscles. He quickly crossed to Niko and handed him Uri. "Go, take Ana and Uri back to Markus. I don't care what he's doing. Have him take the children to Jonathan if you have to. Just get them out of here."

Vaska was grateful when Niko nodded and did as he said instead of arguing. He didn't have time to coddle Niko or play nice. Serge was about to explode, and Vaska needed to be able to focus all of his attention on the man when it happened.

This was a dangerous situation, made even more so if Ana was correct. Although, Vaska couldn't see how she could be. He couldn't imagine Serge being a wolf anymore than he could his suspicion that the man might be mated to him and Niko.

None of this made sense.

The moment the door closed behind Niko and the children, Vaska turned his attention fully on the man sitting on the bed. Serge's skin had turned a pale, pasty white. His milky blue eyes looked dazed and dominated his face. He was slowly shaking his head.

"Serge—"

"Why would she say something like that?"

"She's a child, Serge. I doubt she knew what she was saying."

Serge shook his head. His eyes were agonized when he turned them up to Vaska. "She knew exactly what she was saying."

Vaska could see Serge starting to come apart at the seams. He didn't understand how the words spoken by a small child could have such an impact on the man when his didn't even make a dent.

"Serge—"

"I'm not a monster," Serge whispered. "I'm not."

Vaska debated whether to pursue that statement for about half a second then decided it wasn't worth it. Serge didn't need Vaska arguing with him over whether werewolves were monsters or not, not at the moment. His world had just been rocked by a four-year-old little girl. That's what they needed to deal with right now.

"Would it be so bad being a wolf?"

"Yes!"

"Why?"

"Because…because…" Serge's lips pressed together until they turned white.

Vaska walked over and sat on the side of the bed. He watched Serge carefully just in case his agonized appearance and attitude were all an act. He wouldn't put it past the man. He'd seen worse.

"Being a wolf is not horrible, Serge."

"How can you say that?" Serge gasped. "You're killers. You have no control over your emotions. You kill without thought. You're ruled by the phases of the moon. You shift into something not human."

"We can also smell the rain hours before it falls, taste scent in the air, and hear things from great distances. We have a bond with our families and our packs that is unlike anything you've ever experienced. We're one large family."

"Which explains why Ana's alpha killed her parents."

"Serge, even you can admit that there are bad people in the world. It doesn't matter if they are wolves or humans. They exist. We normally don't act in that manner, and that was an isolated case. But it does happen as it does in the human world."

Serge frowned. "That doesn't mean I'm a wolf or that hunters killed my family."

"No, it doesn't, but can you honestly say it's not possible?"

"I don't know." Serge rubbed his hands over his face then dropped them into his lap. "I remember my mother crying as she hid me and my twin brother. She told us to stay put, but my brother got scared and went to try and find her."

Vaska could see the anguish in Serge's eyes as the man relived his memories. "What happened then, Serge?"

"There was a lot of screaming and crying, yelling." Serge's forehead wrinkled as if the memory was playing out before his eyes. "I waited until the noise stopped. When I came out, there was blood everywhere. My family was dead."

"I want you to think real hard, Serge. How did your family die?"

"They were killed."

"No, I mean, how did they die? Exactly how? Were they stabbed? Ripped apart? Bitten? How did they die?" Vaska hated to ask, but knowing how Serge's family died might give him a clue into who killed them.

"Um…my father was hung upside down from a tree in our front yard. His throat had been cut." Serge frowned. "My brother was on the living room floor. I don't know how he died. I couldn't tell. There was no blood. He looked like he was sleeping."

"And your mother?" Vaska asked when Serge stopped speaking.

"She was upstairs in the bedroom. They tied her down to the bed and…and…"

"It's okay." Vaska grimaced. "I get the picture."

"Her eyes were open, and she just kept staring at me. I thought she was alive at first, and I tried to untie her, but I was just a child, barely five years old. I wasn't strong enough. It wasn't until the others arrived that I realized she was dead."

"Others? What others?"

"The hunters."

"How long were you with your mother before the hunters arrived?"

"I don't know." Serge shrugged. "It felt like hours, but it could have been just a few minutes."

Vaska didn't want to tell Serge that the people that raised him had most likely killed his family. He wasn't sure the man could take it in his present state of mind. However, he was positive that wolves hadn't killed Serge's mother, father, and brother.

"Serge, I know you probably won't believe me, but I want you to listen to me carefully. If wolves had attacked your family, they would not have died the way they did, and you would not have survived it."

"How—" Serge swallowed hard. "How do you know? You weren't there."

"No, I wasn't. But think about it logically. If wolves did indeed kill your father, do you really think they would have slit his throat, or would they have ripped it out with their teeth? And what about your brother? You said there was no blood. Are you sure he was even dead?"

"Of course he's dead!" Serge snapped. "He would be with me if he wasn't dead."

"Maybe and maybe not, but what if he escaped? Or was taken and raised somewhere else? Have you ever considered that?"

"I've visited his grave!" Serge shouted. His hands gripped the blankets until his knuckles turned white.

"But did you see him get buried?"

"No, but…"

"We have a very strong sense of smell, Serge. If you had been hiding and wolves attacked your home, they would have sniffed you out. There would be no place you could have hid. Wolves would have found you and killed you if that was their intent."

Serge glared. "Fine, what if everything you're saying is true. What does it mean?"

"It means that you were lied to. Wolves didn't attack your family and kill them."

"Then who did?" Serge shouted. "Who killed my family?"

"I don't know, Serge, but I may be able to find out."

"How?" Serge eyed Vaska warily.

"I have a friend that occasionally gets me information when I ask for it. I can call him. I just need to know where and when your family was attacked."

"We lived outside of Kozhva, along the Pechora River," Serge said quietly. "It was about twenty-five years ago."

Vaska nodded as he stood up and pulled his cell phone out of his pocket. "What was the name of your pack?"

"How the hell would I know?"

"Okay, then what were the names of your parents?"

"Mom and Dad?"

"Serge, please. I'm just trying to help here. The more information that I have to give Siro, the better chance we have of him finding something."

Serge sighed deeply and fell back against the pillows behind him. "I don't remember much about them, really, just glimpses. I think Dad called my Mom Natya or Natalia, something like that. He was called Marius or Remus, something."

"Marius or Remus?" The two names were at opposite ends of the spectrum. "Are you sure?"

Serge shrugged. "I remember both being spoken in the house when I was a child. I just can't remember which one was my father's name. I suppose the other name could have been a relative or a friend of the family or something."

Vaska nodded and dialed Siro's number. He got a recording and decided to leave a message. He knew it was a secure mailbox and only Siro would hear him, otherwise he would have just hung up.

"Siro, I need you to track down some information for me on a family named Dmitriev that lived outside of Kozhva, along the Pechora River about twenty-five years ago. Mother was named Natya or Natalia. Father's name could be Remus or Marius. Two sons, one named Serge and the other named…uh…" Vaska glanced over at Serge. "What was your brother's name?"

"Yurok," Serge replied. "He was my twin brother."

"Okay, the brothers were Serge and Yurok, twins. They would have been about five years old at the time. I need to know everything you can find out about this family. They may or may not have been attacked and killed by hunters or other wolves. And I need this as soon as you can get it to me. Thanks, Siro."

Vaska snapped the phone closed and turned to look at Serge. "Why don't we get you something to wear, and then we can go downstairs and eat. I'm sure Markus has whipped us up something nutritious, although I can't swear to how it will taste. Markus hasn't been cooking very long, but he tries."

"Why are you doing this?" Serge asked quietly. "Nothing has changed since I woke up. I'm still going to kill you."

"You can try," Vaska said as he walked over to his dresser. He guessed Serge's height to be a couple of inches taller than him, so he grabbed some sweat pants and a cotton shirt, tossing them on the bed next to Serge.

"You're crazy."

Vaska crossed his arms over his chest and leaned back against his dresser. He smirked at the astonished look on Serge's face. "More than likely."

"Aren't you worried about what I might do to Niko or those children?" Serge slapped his hands on the blankets. "I'm a hunter. I've already attacked you and your little mate once. What's to keep me from doing it again?"

Vaska rolled his eyes and pushed himself away from the dresser. He had no idea what suddenly possessed him when he crossed the room and opened a small drawer on his nightstand. He pulled out a sharp knife and handed it to Serge then sat down on the bed and turned around until his back was to Serge.

"So, kill me already."

"You think I won't?" Serge growled.

Vaska tried to keep his breathing even when he felt Serge's body press against him from behind, the blade of the knife pressed against his throat in the front. Serge's breath blew unevenly across his cheek.

"Do you think I won't kill you, wolf?" Serge whispered in his ear. "Do you think I won't slit your throat at the first opportunity? I've spent the majority of my life insuring that your kind is wiped from the face of the earth."

Vaska reached up and wrapped his fingers around Serge's wrist and hand, the one holding the knife. He pressed it closer to his throat until he felt a small trickle of blood drip down his neck.

"Then now is your big chance, hunter." Vaska pressed harder. "Kill me."

Serge's hand began to tremble. Vaska could feel the inner struggle the man fought. Everything he learned, everything he had been taught, told him to bring the knife across Vaska's throat and kill him. Only a deep inner instinct prevented Serge from following through with what he thought he needed to do. At least, that's what Vaska hoped was going on. He could be wrong.

"I thought you were going to kill me, hunter. I'm right here." Vaska pointed to the French doors off to one side of the bed. "Those doors lead to a small courtyard. You can escape through them and sneak out into the countryside before anyone can catch you. What are you waiting for, Serge?"

Serge struggled against Vaska's hold, pulling away. The moment his hand swung free, he tossed the knife across the room and scooted away from Vaska. When Vaska turned to look at the man, he was pressed up against the headboard. Horror paled his face.

"You're out of your mind."

"You keep swearing that you're going to kill me, Serge. I was just giving you the opportunity to do what you said you were going to do."

"You really want me to kill you?"

"It seems to be what you want." Vaska waved his hand absently into the air. "It's all you've been talking about since you woke up. I was just giving you the opportunity."

Serge started slowly shaking his head. "You're really crazy," he whispered. "I thought you were just being an ass, but you really are crazy."

Vaska chuckled. "Well, that's one way to look at it."

"It's the only way to look at it," Serge said as he moved to the far side of the bed away from Vaska. "You're off your fucking rocker, man."

He grabbed the clothes Vaska had tossed at them and quickly pulled them on, but not so fast that Vaska didn't get a good look at his muscular body. The man really was very well built. If he ever shifted, he'd be quite impressive.

"Well, we can discuss that later." Vaska chuckled as he climbed to his feet. "I don't know about you, but I'm hungry. I haven't eaten since yesterday. Why don't we go downstairs and see what Markus has cooked up for us?"

Serge's head titled to one side and his eyes narrowed. "Why are you being so calm about all of this?"

"I see no reason to panic. You've made yourself very clear. I've made myself very clear. I think we understand each other perfectly. Besides, I don't like to get into intense conversation before I've had my coffee. Muddles the brain, you know."

Vaska pressed his lips together to keep from laughing as he turned away from Serge and headed for the door. It seemed to him that keeping Serge questioning things was the only way to go. Off-kilter, Serge was much easier to deal with.

He could hear Serge mumbling to himself as he followed, his bare feet smacking softly on the hardwood floors. Vaska felt a definite bounce of excitement in his steps as he went down the stairs. His day was looking better already.

"We're coming down, majiktoka," Vaska said to Niko through their bond. *"Are you ready for us?"*

"We're already in the dining room."

"We'll be right there."

Vaska stopped suddenly and swung around when Serge cried out, grabbing his head with his hands. He watched the man's legs start to buckle and ran back up the stairs toward him, wrapping his arms around Serge's waist before he could hit the floor.

"Niko, stairs. I need help." he shouted silently.

A moment later he heard a door downstairs slam against a wall and the loud pounding of someone running. Vaska started to lower Serge to the floor then felt someone else brush against him, helping him.

"What happened?" Niko asked as he knelt on the floor and cradled Serge's head in his lap.

"I don't know. One minute he was fine, following right behind me. The next, he cried out and started to go down."

"Could he have internal injuries or something?"

"No, I checked for that earlier when we were undressing him and cleaning him up. Except for some bruises and abrasions, he was fine."

"Then what's happened to him?"

"I don't know, Nikolai." Vaska realized he had snapped at Niko as soon as the man leaned back from him, his eyebrows drawing together. He regretted his words instantly. He quickly held up his hand. "I'm sorry, majiktoka, I should not have shouted at you. I'm just worried."

"I know, Vaska." Niko's face softened. "I'm worried as well."

"Could it be the mating?" Vaska switched to talking to Niko through their bond in case Serge was playing them again. There were some things he wasn't quite ready to discuss with the man yet.

"Vaska, we don't know for sure he's mated to us."

"Niko, you know and I know it. The only one who doesn't know it is Serge." Vaska gestured to Serge with a wave of his hand. *"Look*

how much better he looks already? I only bit him a little while ago. I imagine if you were to bite him as well he'd be back in perfect shape in no time."

"If that's true, Vaska, you know what this means, don't you?"

"Yeah, our wolf hunter is a Tri Omega."

Niko rolled his eyes. *"He's going to be so pleased."*

"Are you kidding me? He's going to be pissed." Vaska snickered. *"He might actually come through with his promise after he finds out and kill us both."*

"He's not going to like it, that's for sure." Niko gently brushed the hair back from Serge's face. *"Any idea how we're going to tell him?"*

"Not a one." Vaska grimaced. *"I was kind of trying to bring him into our world slowly, but if he's already passing out, that may not be an option."*

"If I remember correctly, once we've bitten him, he needs both of us to claim him on a regular basis or he'll die. Four or five days, wasn't it?"

Vaska nodded.

"Well, that's about what it's been since he attacked me, give or take a day. I know you've bitten him, and that seems to have done him some good, but maybe he needs me to bite him as well."

"So, bite him then."

"You'd like it to be that easy, wouldn't you?"

"Niko, you—"

"Would you please stop shouting," a loud voice said from below them. "My head is splitting."

Vaska glanced down in shock to find Serge holding his head between his hands. His eyes were squeezed tight. Serge's face was pale again, his eyebrows drawn down in a deep frown as if he were in a lot of pain.

"Serge, are you okay?" Vaska asked out loud.

"Better yet, can he hear us talking?" Niko asked mentally.

"Hell yes, I can hear you talking and no, I'm not okay. My head feels like it's about to explode."

Vaska blinked over at Niko. He wanted to ask Niko if he knew what was going on, but he was afraid of making Serge hurt any more than he was. It was clear to Vaska, and probably Niko, too, that Serge could hear them talking through their mate bond.

It made sense. Both Vaska and Niko had bitten Serge at some point. The mating bond had taken a hold of all of them. It was only a matter of time before they couldn't be separated for any length of time, if it hadn't happened already.

If Serge didn't accept them, they were fucked.

"Serge, do you think you can get up?" Vaska asked.

"Of course I can get up," Serge snapped as he struggled to his feet. "I may be human, but I'm not an invalid."

"You also may not be human."

Vaska wished he'd kept his mouth shut almost as soon as the words were out of his mouth. Serge's face closed up, and he jerked away. The stiffness of the man's shoulder added with the clench of his jaw told Vaska Serge wasn't happy.

"I am not one of you!"

"We've talked about this, Serge," Vaska said. "Being a wolf is not that bad, and you need to consider that it's a very real possibility."

"No!"

"You know," Niko said, "for someone that doesn't like yelling, you certainly seem to be doing an awful lot of it."

"What would you know?"

"I know a lot," Niko said, crossing his arms over his chest. "Right about now you feel so confused you don't know which way is up. Your head feels like it's about to explode because there's a constant buzzing inside that won't go away."

With each word Niko spoke, Serge's eyes widened even more.

"The scents around you are becoming more intense. You can smell the rain storm that is coming in from the north." Niko rubbed his hand over his jaw as he glanced out the window. "I'd say it should be here in about four hours. Does that feel about right, Vaska?"

"Just about."

"The sounds you hear are becoming stronger, almost like you can hear the blades of grass growing outside. If you listen real carefully, you might even be able to hear a dog barking off in the distance. I'd estimate he's no more than one or two miles away."

Serge's brow furrowed. "He's barking a lot. He sounds really upset."

"So, you can hear him then," Niko said. "Do you hear the car that is drowning out his barking? It's coming closer."

The milky blue in Serge's eyes suddenly bled out, leaving them eerily white. His voice sounded husky when he spoke, almost as if coming from far off. "It's a blue car, two people inside. They're coming here."

Vaska glanced at Niko to see the same surprise he felt plastered all over his mate's face. He wiggled his eyebrows and nodded toward Serge. Niko just shrugged his shoulders and looked back at Serge.

"How do you know they are coming here, Serge?" Niko asked softly.

"I can see them," Serge said. "I can hear them."

"What are they saying?"

"They're talking about you, Niko." Serge frowned. "Something about the Triad of Trouble."

Vaska arched an eyebrow when Niko started chuckling. He'd have to ask Niko about that but later, much later. First they needed to figure out what was going on with Serge.

"There's someone else coming too."

"Someone else?" Vaska asked. "Who?"

"I don't know, but I think I should. There's something about him, something…"

"Something, Serge?" Vaska asked.

"He's…he's…"

Serge suddenly started shaking. Vaska and Niko stepped forward and caught Serge right before he crashed to the floor. Vaska looked up at Niko in surprised. "What in the hell was that all about?"

"I think our Tri Omega is coming into his powers."

Chapter 11

Niko leaned against the bedpost as Vaska tucked Serge in. He smiled at the care Vaska took with a man that professed to want to kill them both at the first opportunity. There were deeper depths to Vaska than he had expected. Niko wanted to explore them.

Hell, he wanted to explore everything about Vaska. The man fascinated him on every level, and that made Niko want to laugh long and loud. He never expected to be mated, and he suddenly found himself with two. Didn't that just beat all?

"What are you smiling at?" Vaska asked as he stood up straight and walked to the end of the bed to stand next to him.

"You."

"Me?"

"How many times has Serge threatened to kill us?"

"More times than I can count, but he won't do it."

"You're sure of that?"

"I am."

Niko stepped closer to Vaska, moving into the natural curve of the man's body. "How can you be so sure?"

"He already feels the mating bond even if he doesn't want to admit it. He'd no more kill us then he would cut off his arm."

Niko leaned into the hand Vaska stroked down the side of his face, amazed at how much that simple touch filled him with joy. "He's going to be a hard nut to crack. You realize that, don't you?"

Niko didn't want Vaska to get his hopes up only to have them dashed away. Matings weren't perfect. Just because the bond was there didn't mean that things would work out for the mates. The bond just gave them a starting point.

At least, that's how Niko felt. He didn't know how Vaska felt, or Serge. Niko knew that the three of them had a lot of road to go before things were perfect between them. They weren't exactly starting out on the best footing.

Niko was terrified of being committed and having the responsibility of someone else's life in his care. Vaska couldn't admit that he needed someone, anyone. He was too used to standing on his own.

And Serge, he didn't even know he was mated. Niko was a little afraid of what would happen when he did find out. There was a very real possibility that Serge would totally freak and leave both him and Vaska.

It would kill him, but Niko wasn't sure the man would care. He seemed to hate wolves that much. Finding out that not only was he a wolf but a special Tri Omega wolf was sure to throw Serge's world into turmoil.

"How are you feeling about all of this, majiktoka? I know you never wanted to be mated in the first place, and now you have two. Are you going to be able to handle that?"

Niko could hear the vulnerability in Vaska's voice. He could see it in the man's deep blue eyes. Vaska was terrified of being rejected again. Niko felt about an inch tall when he realized he had been the one to put that fear into Vaska's eyes.

"I'm a little shocked, I'll admit that," Niko said. "But I'm not sorry, not now that I feel what we can have together."

"Even if you have two mates? That means a whole lot of responsibility."

Niko smiled. Vaska was coming to know him so well, and it had just been a few days. There was something a little scary in that and something more that pulled at Niko's heart strings. He liked knowing his mate knew him.

Niko pushed closer to Vaska and brushed his hands down the man's solid chest. "We stand together, the three of us. That's enough."

"We still don't know if Serge will stand with us, Niko. You need to be aware of that."

"No, I don't. He could try and kill us even after he knows everything. I just have to have the hope that he won't, that he'll want us as much as we want him."

"I want you." Vaska's hand stroked down the side of Niko's face again. "I think I've always wanted you."

Niko suddenly couldn't breathe. Vaska did it to him every time. The man simply had to say something sexy and Niko was panting after him. "Is it always going to be like this, Vaska?"

"Between you and me it is."

"What about him?" Niko asked as he nodded toward the bed where Serge lay unconscious. "Do you think it will be that way with him?"

"How could it not?" Vaska asked. "Fate wouldn't be cruel enough to mate us to someone we couldn't be happy with."

"Hell, who cares about being happy?" Niko snorted. "I'm just worried about us being compatible in bed."

"Niko!" Vaska asked.

"What? Like you weren't thinking the same thing."

Vaska chuckled, his face flushing.

"You were," Niko said.

"Have you looked at Serge? Of course I've been thinking about what we'd all be like in bed." Vaska wiggled his eyebrows. "I got to see him naked when he was getting dressed. You'd be thinking the same thing."

"You got to see him naked, and you didn't call me?" Niko sucked in a breath as images began to build in his mind, making him feel achy. "What did he look like?"

"Hot!"

"Yeah?"

"Oh yeah."

Niko dropped his head forward against Vaska's chest. "Oh, I am so jealous." He looked up when Vaska suddenly stilled. "What?"

"We can't be jealous of each other, Niko. That's the quickest way to rip us apart."

"I know that."

"There will be times when only two of us are together and times when all of us are together. You know that, right?"

Niko quickly grabbed Vaska's face with his hands. "Honey, I have a lot of experience being around mated Tri Omegas. I know how it works. We're better together than apart, but together does not mean there won't be occasions when two of us are together instead of all three of us. As long as we take strides to make sure everyone is included as often as possible and that everyone feels that they are part of the relationship, we'll be fine."

"Do you think that's possible?"

"Oh yeah." Niko chuckled. "You should see some of my friends. I swear they spend more time fucking in the bathroom than they do showering. They seem to go out of their way to find time for all of them to be together."

"I just worry, Niko. I thought I'd die when you said you didn't want me. If I lost both of you..." Vaska shook his head. "I think I'd beg the hunters to kill me."

Niko could see the damage his thoughtless reaction to their mating had done to the big self-assured man and wanted to scream in frustration. He'd almost lost something so important and all because he was afraid. Now, he was afraid he'd never be able to undo the hurt he had inflicted on Vaska.

"I'm so sorry, Vaska," Niko whispered. He planted a series of small kisses along Vaska's strong jaw line. "I swear on my life I will never deny you again. And I will spend the rest of my life proving it to you if you'll let me."

"Just accept me now," Vaska murmured back. "That's all I want."

Niko grabbed Vaska's face again, tilting the taller man's head down so he could look deep into his blue eyes. He wanted Vaska to know he spoke the absolute truth. "I do accept you, Vasiliy. I accept you as my mate, today and always. You will never have cause to doubt me again."

"Yeah?" he asked unevenly, his voice hitching. His eyes filled.

Niko suddenly realized that as strong and powerful as Vaska was, there was a little part of him that craved being accepted, wanted. Niko's rejection of their mating only added to that, making Vaska unsure of everything else.

Niko remembered all of the things Vaska had told him about hiding in the secret passages while trying to escape his father and brother, and everything suddenly made sense to him. Vaska had been rejected by everyone important to him in his life. He sort of expected it. Niko needed to change that starting now.

"I can't speak for Serge, Vaska. I'm not him, and I don't know him well enough to say how he is going to react to all of this. But no matter what happens with him, you will always have me. I will not leave you. I will not betray you. And I will not stop being here for you. We're mates, Vaska, and that means everything to me."

Niko saw Vaska's eyes widen in surprise. He was a little surprised himself, not at his words, but how much he really meant them. He never expected to actually speak those words to someone or to feel so right saying them.

Niko knew he had said the right thing when a smile began to spread across Vaska's mouth, lighting up his face. It was a very good look on the big man. Niko swore to himself he'd do everything in his power to see that look on Vaska's face as often as he could.

"How about I start proving it right now?" Niko asked as he let go of Vaska's face and dropped to his knees, reaching for the buttons on the man's jeans.

"N-now?" Vaska gasped. "Right now?"

"Yep," Niko said as he went to work on getting Vaska's pants open and his cock out.

"Wha-what about Serge?"

"He can join in if he wants to."

"Niko!"

Niko tilted his head back and looked up at Vaska. "Do you want me to stop?"

Vaska swallowed. "No, but..."

Niko smirked and went back to what he was doing. He didn't know a man alive that would turn down a blow job. He knew Vaska wouldn't. Niko quickly undid Vaska's pants then pulled them down to his thighs. The man's thick, hard cock bounced free right in front of him.

"Niko, wait."

Niko was shocked. "You want me to stop?"

"I'd rather cut off my arm, but I haven't had a shower since this morning."

Niko groaned as he dropped his head forward against Vaska's thigh. He was grateful the man had stopped him since he hadn't had a shower, but he so wanted to feel Vaska come in his mouth.

"I could go shower real quick."

Niko chuckled and shook his head. "We have company on the way. I don't think there's enough time. However..."

He stood up and reached for the buttons on his jeans. He was grateful he hadn't put on shoes yet today when he was able to push his pants down his legs and off his feet. A quick lifting and toss of his shirt had him standing naked in front of Vaska.

He reached down and grabbed the bottle of lube out of his pocket and handed it to Vaska then turned and grabbed the bottom bed frame. Niko spread his legs and pushed his ass out, displaying himself for his mate. He glanced over his shoulder at Vaska, laughing softly when he found the man's eyes pinned on his ass.

"If you're quick, we can still fool around."

"I can be quick."

Niko had no doubt the man could be quick, but he was a little surprised at the swiftness in which Vaska stepped forward, lubed up his fingers, and shoved two of them into his ass. He gripped the footboard tighter and inhaled sharply at the bite of pain that he felt. Luckily, it faded fast, replaced by complete and utter bliss as Vaska started moving his fingers in and out.

Once again, Niko was mystified by his willingness to bottom for someone. He was actually starting to look forward to being fucked by Vaska. He never thought he'd feel that way in his life. Being mated was a constant surprise.

"Quicker than that, Vaska."

Niko braced himself, knowing what his words would do to the powerful man. He wasn't wrong. A third lubed finger pushed into his ass along with the first two. Niko could feel his own cock bouncing wildly in front of him at the force Vaska used when thrusting his fingers in then pulling them out.

He almost wished for a flat surface so he could get on his hands and knees and reach under his body to stroke his cock, almost. Vaska was pretty damn good at giving him every last ounce of pleasure his body could sustain. The man seemed to know just how hard to push, when to pull out, and what to touch in between.

"Now, Vaska," Niko whispered hoarsely.

"Yeah, now."

When Vaska pulled his fingers out, Niko arched up onto his tip toes and stuck his ass out even more. His silent invitation was answered when Vaska grabbed his hips and drove in with such force that Niko hit the bed frame.

Niko opened his mouth to speak at the same moment Vaska started moving. All that came out was a long cry as Vaska nailed his prostate with the first stroke then every stroke after that. Niko's level of pleasure went from moderate to overboard in a matter of moments.

He was filled so fully each and every time that he didn't think he would need to even touch his cock before coming. He could already feel drops of pre-cum dripping down his throbbing cock and his balls drawing up tight against his body.

He could hear the bed creaking as Vaska hammered into his ass over and over again. He also heard a low groan that didn't come from behind him and quickly looked up to the head of the bed. Milky blue eyes blinked back at him, looking a little stunned.

Niko grinned as he watched Serge reach under the blankets. A moment later, the blanket covering Serge started quickly moving up and down as the man stroked his cock. Serge's eyes never left Niko and Vaska.

"You like my ass, Vaska?"

"Damn, Niko!" Vaska groaned. "Your ass was made to be fucked."

"Do you think Serge would enjoy fucking my ass?" Niko arched an eyebrow at Serge when the man's eyes widened considerably. "Maybe he'd enjoy it more if I fucked his ass?"

"Oh yeah, majiktoka," Vaska groaned. "I want to see you fuck Serge's ass. That would be so sweet."

Serge was breathing so hard that Niko was a little worried the man might pass out. His chest rose and fell at a rapid rate. The hand he stroked his cock with moved even faster.

"I bet he has a tight ass, Vaska."

"Fuck, yes!" Vaska started thrusting harder, faster. His hands dug into Niko's hips.

Niko started panting. His cock throbbed. He ached, and each thrust of Vaska's cock in his ass only made him ache more. "Vaska, please," he groaned. He needed to come so bad he could feel it in the shaking of his body.

Vaska's hand suddenly wrapped around Niko's cock. At the same moment, Vaska's canines sank into the vulnerable skin between

Niko's neck and shoulder. Niko cried out and tilted his head to one side to give Vaska better access. He didn't take his eyes off of Serge.

"Serge is watching us, Vaska," Niko whispered through their bond. *"Can you see him? Can you see how much he enjoys watching you fuck my ass?"*

Vaska's thrusts stuttered for a moment then suddenly sped up. Niko inhaled sharply when Vaska's claws started to dig into the skin of his hip. Knowing Serge watched them was arousing Vaska to a fever pitch. Niko could feel it in the wild way Vaska fucked him and the emotions coming through their bond. Vaska liked being watched.

Niko tucked that bit of information away for use at a later date and concentrated on being fucked by one mate and watched by the other. He knew Serge was getting close to coming when the man suddenly kicked the blankets off of his body. His hand gripped his cock so tightly the head was purple and leaking.

"I need up on the bed, Vaska. I want to suck Serge's cock."

"Fuck, you're going to kill me," Vaska groaned, but he followed Niko up onto the bed.

Vaska moved with Niko, never pulling his cock out, as they got situated on the bed, Niko on his hands and knees, Vaska kneeling behind him. Niko was hesitant about approaching Serge until the man spread his legs. Niko quickly crawled between them.

He kept his eyes connected to Serge's as he slowly lowered his head and enveloped the head of the man's cock. Serge's hand fell away, and Niko swallowed him down to the root. The soft moan of ecstasy that fell from Serge's lips was music to Niko's ears.

"Oh sweet hell!" Serge cried out. "You're mouth is fucking perfect."

"His ass is better," Vaska said.

"Oh fuck!"

Niko grinned as he felt Serge's hands clenched in his hair. He stuck two of his fingers into his mouth, getting them wet then moved them down between Serge's ass cheeks. He sucked Serge's cock down into his mouth at the same time he pushed his fingers into the man's ass. He groaned as warm silk enclosed his fingers, gripping him like they never wanted to leave.

Serge was humping his hips into the air then moving back, impaling his ass on Niko's fingers. Niko knew from the desperate sounds falling from Serge's mouth that the man was starving for affection. He needed so bad that Niko almost cried.

Niko moved a third finger into Serge's ass the next time he thrust them in. He pounded his fingers in and out of Serge's tight hole as fast as Vaska was fucking him. Knowing he was bringing both of his mates pleasure was beyond anything Niko had ever felt in his life. He felt strong, powerful.

"Lube, honey."

Niko held out his hand behind him. A moment later, the small bottle of lube was slapped into his hand. Niko quickly coated his fingers as he pulled them out of Serge's ass then thrust them back in. Serge's cries became louder, his movements more forceful.

"Please, please, I need…" Serge groaned.

"I know what you need, honey," Niko said silently, pushing the words into Serge's mind through their bond.

Serge's eyes widened even more than before, but Niko didn't think it came from the man hearing him in his mind. Niko was pretty sure it came from him pulling his fingers out of Serge's ass and kneeling up between his thighs.

Niko lifted Serge's legs over his arms and moved his hips until his cock pushed against the tight circle of muscles guarding Serge's ass. He raised his eyes to Serge's. He wanted to fuck Serge more than he wanted his next breath, but he wouldn't force the man.

"Do you want me to fuck you, Serge?"

Serge licked his lips. He looked a little unsure, a little freaked out. His eyes darted around the room landing on Niko and Vaska several times then looking away. His hands clenched then unclenched.

"I'll just suck you off if that's what you want, Serge."

Niko started to lower Serge's legs back down to the bed, disappointment filling every corner of his body as he did, but it was tempered by the uncertainty and fear he could feel coming from Serge. The man was unsettled by everything that was happening and Niko couldn't fault him for that.

"No."

Niko glanced up. "No?"

He could feel Vaska's body still behind him.

"I...you..." Serge's eyes seemed to beseech Niko for some kind of understanding.

"What do you need, Serge?"

"Fuck me!"

"Anything you want." Niko gripped Serge's thighs again, surging upward into Serge's ass so fast that Vaska's cock was almost dislodged from his own ass. He didn't want to give Serge time to change his mind.

The triple groans that filled the room as all three men found themselves connected together at the same moment was one Niko would never forget, not as long as he lived. He finally understood why all of his friends worked so hard to be together at the same time. There was nothing on earth like fucking one mate while being fucked by the other one.

"Move, majiktoka," Vaska groaned in his ear.

Niko grinned as he started pushing into Serge's tight heat. It took him a moment and a few sharp claws digging into his hips before Niko found the rhythm that Vaska wanted him on. He thrust into Serge as Vaska pulled back. He pulled out of Serge as Vaska thrust in.

It was the perfect symphony of movements.

"Soon, majiktoka."

"Yes."

Niko dropped one of Serge's legs then reached down and grabbed his cock, stroking him quickly. Serge's legs started to tremble as he stiffened, the muscles going tight. Niko knew the man was as close to orgasm as him and Vaska.

"Gonna come in your ass, Serge."

Serge nodded rapidly. His eyes were narrowed on Niko's hand wrapped around his cock. He kept licking his lips in between heavy pants. There was a flush to his skin as if his body was heated from the inside out.

"Next time"—Niko panted—"next time you can come in my ass."

That seemed to be all Serge needed to send him over the edge. His inner muscles clamped down around Niko's cock as his body arched up into the air, his head falling back and pressing back into the pillow.

Niko groaned as hot seed covered his hand. Watching Serge come was glorious. Feeling him come was even better. Serge's body gripped Niko's cock like a tight silken glove, massaging him and dragging his climax from him.

Niko thrust as deeply into Serge as their bodies would allow and let the sensations rocking his body take him. His cock pulsed and swelled. Just as he started to empty himself into Serge's snug body, Niko leaned forward and sank his teeth into the skin over Serge's heart. He heard Serge cry out and more hot seed covered his hand.

Behind him, Vaska suddenly stiffened, his entire body going bowstring tight. He thrust into Niko once more, almost to the point of pain. Niko groaned as Vaska's release filled him. He could feel each throb of the man's cock in his ass.

After a moment, Vaska slumped down over the top of him. The man's sweaty head came to rest in the middle of Niko's back. Niko withdrew his teeth from Serge's chest and licked the small bite mark clean.

Happiness filled him on a level he couldn't put into words. He lifted his head and looked up at Serge, wanting to share his joy with both of his mates. What he found made the delight in his heart start to dwindle away. He imagined it was much like what Vaska felt when he denied their mating, and he wanted to cry for the pain he had caused his mate. Only, he was too close to crying because of his own pain.

Serge stared up at him with a look of shock and horror on his face. His eyes were so wide that they almost dominated his pale face. Niko pushed himself up then pulled out of Serge. He reached back with one hand and grabbed Vaska's arm, leaning back against his larger body.

"Serge?"

Chapter 12

Horror laced every thought flying through Serge's mind as he realized he had just participated in a three way ménage with two wolves, his sworn enemies. Not only had he participated, he had begged to be fucked.

It went against everything he had ever been taught, everything he had ever known. So, why did it feel so good, and why did he want to do it again? Why did the mere thought of never feeling Niko's cock in his ass or experiencing Vaska fucking him fill him with such dread?

"I…I need to use the bathroom."

Vaska pointed to a door on the far wall. "Right through there."

Serge nodded and rolled to the side of the bed. He saw Vaska's arms wrap around Niko out of the corner of his eye as he grabbed his clothes off the floor and sprinted across the room. The bathroom door slammed behind him. Serge quickly turned and locked it then leaned his head against the cold wood.

He had lost his mind. He had just had sex with two wolves, and he enjoyed it. And he wanted to do it again. And…Serge shook his head. He had definitely lost his mind. If any other hunter ever learned what he had done, they would kill him on sight.

Serge pushed himself away from the door and walked over to the sink. He found a clean washcloth in a stack on the counter and cleaned himself up. He tossed the washcloth in a nearby hamper then rested his hands on the countertop and looked at himself in the mirror.

He didn't look any different. Same milky blue eyes, same sunlight-blond hair. Nothing was out of place. Not even the teeth marks in his chest or on his neck fazed him. Serge breathed in deeply as he remembered Niko biting him when he climaxed. He remembered Vaska biting him when he attacked Niko.

He wasn't stupid enough to think he would suddenly sprout hair and pointed ears, maybe a tail. He'd been a hunter long enough to know that a simple bite could not pass on the wolf gene. That didn't mean he was exactly okay with either man biting him, but mainly because he had enjoyed it too much.

Serge always had a kink for being bit during sex, and Niko seemed to hone right in on it. He had absolutely no idea how the man had even known, and that scared him. There seemed to be a lot Niko knew about him. That wasn't a good thing.

Serge was supposed to be here to kill Niko and Vaska, not fuck them. He didn't think he would be able to do that now that they had been intimate, especially when he wanted to do it again. And if he didn't kill them, someone else would.

That gave Serge a whole new set of problems. Even if he couldn't bring himself to kill the two wolves, he knew others would be coming for them. The price on Vaska's head alone could set a hunter up for years. Killing Nikolai Miroslav only added to that.

Serge sighed deeply and reached for his clothes. He could hear Niko and Vaska talking softly through the door and knew he'd have to go out and face them at some point. It might be better to get it over and done with.

He needed to lay down the rules to them. No more fucking, no matter what. Serge planned to only be here long enough to find out what Vaska's informant had to say and then he was leaving. He couldn't get involved with them.

Serge quickly pulled his clothes on then stepped toward the door. He took a deep breath then unlocked the door and pulled it open. Serge stepped into the bedroom, his eyes immediately going to the bed.

Fear froze him in his spot for a split second when he saw Niko and Vaska talking to a third man, a man Serge recognized very well.

Adrenaline flooded Serge's bloodstream as rage and anger overshadowed his fear.

He growled low in his throat, the noise growing louder with every second, and lunged across the room. His only thought was to save Niko and Vaska from the wolf hunter standing in front of them.

"Serge, no!" Vaska shouted, but it was too late.

Serge used every bit of his strength and speed to barrel into the man he saw as a threat to Niko and Vaska. He felt the impact of his body hitting the hunter's deep in his bones. Serge shook off the pain and dug his fingers into the hunter's flesh.

He raised his hands to punch him. The feeling of his hands striking against the hunter's vulnerable stomach and face invigorated Serge, spurring him on. There was something about the fight that he gloried in.

"Serge, stop!"

"Serge!"

Serge ignored the voices shouting at him and went after the hunter with more force. He could see a sliver of fear in the hunter's eyes. He knew he was winning. He was protecting Vaska and Niko. Some small inner whisper said he was doing what he was supposed to do.

"Serge, you have to stop!"

Serge growled when he felt strong arms wrap around his neck and pull him away from the hunter. He wanted to kill the hunter. He needed to kill him. Serge couldn't stop thinking that he needed to protect Vaska and Niko. It seemed to be the only thought filtering through the red haze surrounding his mind.

He wanted blood.

Serge swung around and snapped at arms holding him back. He watched Vaska jump back, his arms falling to his sides. Satisfied that Vaska wasn't going to stop him, Serge turned his attention back to the hunter.

The man was slowly backing away from him, clutching his bloody arm to his chest. His eyes were wide and kept jumping from Serge to the two men behind Serge then back again. Serge growled low in his throat and took another step forward.

"Serge, you have to stop." Once again, Serge felt arms encircle his neck. "Siro is not here to hurt us."

Serge opened his mouth to argue, but all that came out was a loud snarl, loud enough to startle Serge and stop him in his tracks. He opened his mouth again and once again, he heard a snarl. Confused, Serge whimpered, but even that didn't sound right.

He turned to look back at Niko and Vaska, hoping they had answers to why he was hearing what he was hearing, only to slip on the floor. His feet couldn't seem to find purchase on the slick surface. Serge stumbled until he fell down, smacking the bottom of his chin on the hardwood floor.

"Serge, honey," Niko said softly, "slow down. You're not used to this body. It will take you a little while to become accustomed to having four legs instead of two."

Huh? Four legs instead of two? Confused, Serge looked down only to find furry paws where his hands should have been. Fear filled him, and he scampered backwards trying to escape what he was seeing, only, the paws followed him.

Serge whimpered.

"Ssshh, Serge," Niko whispered into his ear, the man's arms wrapping around him. "It's going to be okay. When you attacked Siro, you shifted. You just need to shift back."

Serge shook his head. His eyes narrowed. Serge moved his head back and forth a little slower, watching with shock as a blondish-tan muzzle moved back and forth as he wanted his face to do.

"Shit, this was fucking real," Serge thought.

"This is very real, Serge," came the mental reply from Niko.

Niko sat down in front of Serge and grabbed his face with both hands. Serge had no choice but to look right at the man.

"You listen to me very carefully. You've shifted into your wolf form. To shift back is very simple. You just need to think about what it feels like to have skin, two legs instead of four. Just think, Serge."

Serge closed his eyes and visualized having skin instead of fur, two legs instead of four. He pictured what his body looked like when he was in human form. Serge groaned when his bones popped. The pain was there, but not intense, fading with each passing second.

"There you go, Serge, all back to normal."

Serge almost cried. He'd never be normal again. He was a wolf. He'd be hunted for the rest of his life. He'd be…

Serge's eyes snapped open, and he quickly searched for the man he'd been fighting, finding him standing next to Vaska near the bed. Vaska was wrapping a towel around the man's bleeding arm.

"Hu-hunter!" Serge pointed at the man.

"What?" Niko glanced over his shoulder.

"He's a hunter."

"Who?" Niko asked as he looked back at Serge.

"That man, he's a hunter." Serge grabbed Niko's arm desperately. He had to make Niko understand the danger he was in, they were in. "I've seen him at meetings several times. Hell, I've fought beside him. He's a hunter, Niko."

Niko slowly pushed himself to his feet, putting himself between Serge and the hunter. Serge's heart thundered in his chest. He didn't think it was supposed to be this way. Niko was smaller, granted not by much, but he was still smaller. Serge should be protecting him, and Vaska. That just seemed to be the way it should be.

Serge climbed to his feet, wobbling just a bit as he moved forward to place himself between Niko and the threat in the room. He reached over and grabbed Vaska's arm, yanking the man back away from the hunter. He shoved Vaska behind him to where Niko was then turned to glare at the hunter.

"You need to go. Vaska and Niko are under my protection, and I will kill anyone that tries to harm them." Serge didn't miss the soft inhale of breath he heard behind him, but he kept his attention on the hunter in front of him.

"You're one of them," the hunter said.

"It does appear so," Serge replied.

"You will be hunted now, too."

"I am aware of that."

"And yet you still try to protect them." The hunter tilted his head to the side slightly. "Why?"

"They belong to me." It was the only explanation Serge had to give. He felt an unnatural need to protect Vaska and Niko. It was almost obsessive. He didn't know if it came from his new shifter ability or from the fact that they had been intimate. He just knew he had to protect them.

"Even if I leave, you know others will be coming for them, for you."

"Yes."

"You won't be able to stop them all."

Serge nodded. "I know." And he did. Wolf hunters were a tenacious group. They hunted wolves with a dogged determination, bent on wiping them all from the face of the planet. Serge had just become one of the hunted.

"Would it make you feel any better to know that I am one of you?"

Serge frowned. "I've seen you at gatherings. I know you're one of us…uh…them."

"No, I'm a wolf."

Serge started to chuckle until the man suddenly shifted. One second a man stood before him. The next second a tan-colored wolf stood before Serge. Before he could blink again, the man was back before him.

"How…I've seen you. I've fought with you. How…"

"Not everything is as it seems, Serge," Vaska said as he walked up, settling his hand on Serge's shoulder. "This is the man I called earlier, remember? His name is Siro Castilian. He works undercover for the Eastern European Wolf Council."

"You go undercover with the hunters?"

Siro nodded.

"And no one has ever caught you?"

"Not until now." Siro chuckled.

Serge felt like his legs were going to give out beneath him. Everything he had ever known, ever felt, was being put into question on several different levels, and he didn't know how to deal with it. He walked over to the side of the bed and sat down, dropping his head into his hands.

Serge felt so confused. He had conflicting emotions. Serge spent a majority of his life training to hunt wolves then actually hunting them. He'd even killed a few. Now, he was a wolf, one of the hunted.

On the other hand, there was a kind of freedom in knowing he was a wolf. Serge had always envied the way wolf packs seemed to protect each other, the tight knit group that they were. A small hidden part of him always wanted to be part of that group, and now he was.

"Serge, it's going to be okay."

Serge allowed Niko to pull his hands away from his face. Niko looked concerned, but not freaked out. "You know this is nuts, right?"

Niko chuckled. "I'm sure it seems that way to you."

"You have no idea."

"I believe I can solve some of your confusion."

Serge glanced up at Siro when the man spoke. He still didn't like how close the man stood to Niko and Vaska. He didn't trust him. But under the circumstances, he was willing to listen to what the man had to say.

"I'm listening."

"You were born outside of Kozhva, along Pechora River," Siro began. "You were a twin, your brother being Yurok Dmitriev."

"Well, you certainly seem to know who I am."

"Your mother was Natalya, your fathers Remus and Marius. You—"

"Wait." Serge held up his hand to stop Siro. "My *fathers*? As in plural? I had two fathers?"

"You do not remember?" Siro asked.

Serge frowned, racking his memories, then finally shook his head when he couldn't settle on any single memory of the men that might have been his fathers. "Most of my memories from then are hazy."

"I'm not surprised," Siro said. "You were pretty young when you were taken."

"I was taken?" Shock rolled through Serge and made his hands tremble. He clenched them into fists to hide the fact that he was so affected by Siro's words. "I thought my family was murdered."

"Not exactly." Siro shook his head. "Your brother and one father survived."

"But…but I saw them."

"What exactly did you see, Serge?" Siro asked. "Think hard. You're memories were made through the eyes of a five-year-old child. What did you see that you didn't know you'd seen? What of what you did see was transferred into something more horrific because your mind couldn't process what you were seeing?"

Serge sat back down on the side of the bed and folded his hands together. He didn't really want to relive the murder of his family, not again. Twice in a twenty-four-hour period was more than enough for him.

"We were all sitting around the table eating, and someone knocked on the door. Mother got really upset. She made us hide in the secret hiding spot behind the bathroom cabinet."

"Who is 'we,' Serge?"

"Me and Yurok, my twin brother. We were both in there, but Yurok got scared. We could hear Mother screaming." Serge frowned. "There was a lot of yelling, loud yelling. I thought maybe Mother and

Father were fighting, but they never yelled at each other like that. This was different."

"How so, Serge?" Niko asked. "What was different about it?"

"It sounded angry."

"Isn't all yelling kind of angry?"

"No." Serge shook his head. "This was different. It was...I don't know, hateful angry."

"Did you recognize who was yelling?"

Serge shook his head. "I think I heard the voice before, but I don't know who it belonged to. Father would always make us stay in the house when the man showed up."

"The man?" Niko asked.

"The man with the loud voice. I don't think father liked him very much. He was never invited in—" Serge inhaled sharply. "He was inside the house. That's why I could hear the yelling so well. He was inside the house. Father never let him inside the house."

Siro was suddenly in front of him, squatting down. "This is really important, Serge, can you tell me anything about this man? What he looked like, how he sounded, what he wore? Did you ever hear his name mentioned?"

"No, I just remember that my parents didn't like him very much. Every time he stopped by Mother would rush us off into another room and make us hide. I think she was afraid of him."

"You never saw him?"

Serge shook his head.

"But you're sure he was inside the house?"

"Yeah, he had to be inside the house. The bathroom was at the back of the house, and the secret hiding place was behind the back of the cabinet in the bathroom. It was surrounded by stone in case there was a fire. In order for me to hear him, he had to practically be standing in the bathroom."

"Okay, let's forget about him for a moment, Serge," Siro said. "What else do you remember? Was anyone with this man?"

"There had to be. I heard a lot of voices shouting."

"Did you see anyone?"

"Not until I was rescued."

Serge saw Siro glance up at Vaska for a moment then back at him. "Who rescued you, Serge?"

"The people that raised me, the hunters."

"The hunters." Siro shook his head. "When did they rescue you?"

Serge frowned again as he searched his memories. "Everything went silent. I was scared. I wanted my Mother, Yurok. I slipped out of the hiding space and went looking for them. Yurok was on the living room floor. Father was outside. Mother was upstairs. I stayed with her until the hunters came. I don't know how long it was."

"And you're sure your family was dead?"

"I told you, I saw them. Father was hung upside down from a tree in the front yard. His throat had been cut. Yurok was on the living room floor. I don't know how he died. But Mother, she was the worst. They had tied her down to the bed and…"

"That's enough," Siro said. "You don't have to say anymore."

It wasn't until Siro got up and walked toward the door that Serge saw the small bag lying next to the door. He tensed when Siro bent down to grab his bag, reaching inside to get something. Serge didn't know Siro, and he wasn't about to trust the man.

Siro pulled a large envelope out of his bag and walked back to stand in front of Serge. He opened it up and pulled out a small stack of photographs and started setting them down on the bed beside Serge.

"I want you to look at these pictures, Serge, and tell me if you recognize anyone."

Serge started looking through the pictures. Some were of individuals. Others looked to be family portraits with various numbers of people in them. Some were also old and faded, in black and white, while others were in color.

"Who are these people?" he asked as he leafed through them.

"Just different people from packs around the Pechora River," Siro replied. "Do you recognize anyone?"

"No, not yet," Serge said as he set picture after picture down in a small pile on the mattress. He started to set down an old black and white picture of a man and woman when something about the smile on the woman's face caught his attention. He wasn't sure if it was the lift at each corner of her mouth or the way she smiled, but something about her smile intrigued him.

"She looks familiar."

"What about the man in the picture?"

Serge looked closer. The man in the photograph was a good-looking man, but he didn't hold the same spark of interest as the woman did. Serge shook his head. "No, I don't think I've ever seen him before."

"Look at the others."

Serge set that picture aside and started going through the others. When he came to a picture of two small boys, the air in Serge's lungs seemed to freeze in place. He rubbed his finger gently over first one small face, then the other.

"Serge?"

"This is me."

"And the other boy?"

"Yurok." Serge smiled as a memory assailed him. "I remember when this was taken. It was our fifth birthday party. We got ponies for our birthday. Mine was brown with four white stockings. Yurok's was all black except for one leg. We were so excited."

"So, this is you and your twin brother, Yurok?" Niko asked.

"Yes."

"You don't look much like twins."

"No, we were, we just didn't look alike."

"Do any of the other pictures look familiar?"

Serge frowned as he held up one picture. "This one kind of looks like our house, but I remember it being bigger, much bigger."

Niko chuckled. "I imagine to a five-year-old it was."

Serge looked up at Niko and laughed. "Yeah, I guess it would."

"You said this woman looked familiar to you?" Siro asked as he pointed to the photograph Serge had set aside. Serge turned and looked down at it, nodding.

"Yeah, there's something in her smile." Serge shrugged. "I can't tell you exactly what it is but…"

"How about this picture of her?" Siro asked as he held out another picture. "Can you see the same thing in this picture?"

Serge could see Siro's fingers trembled as he handed the picture over. He started to wonder about that until he looked at the picture and then every other thought left his head. He was looking down at himself, his brother, the man and woman in the precious picture, and a second man. It was a family portrait.

"This is them," he whispered.

"Them?" Siro asked.

"My family, this is them."

"You recognize them all?"

"Yes, this is me." Serge began pointing to the people in the picture. "This is Yurok, my mother, and my father."

"And the other man?"

"He…I don't know who he is, but I think he's supposed to be there." Serge looked up at the three faces looking back at him. "Does that make sense?"

"It does." Siro smiled and pointed to the people in the photograph. "This is Natalya and Marius Dmitriev, and this man right here is Remus. He's your other father."

"My what?"

"Your mother was born a Tri Omega. That meant she needed two mates to keep her grounded and safe. Marius and Remus were her mates."

"A Tri Omega?"

"Tri Omegas are special Omegas, Serge," Niko explained. "They have abilities like healing, telepathy, and the ability to tell if someone is lying or not. Because of their abilities and how rare they are, they need two mates to keep them safe."

"Unfortunately, there is a down side for them," Vaska added. "They are born without a genetic additive that is introduced into their system when they receive the mating bite from their mates. Before then, their bodies don't know they need it. But after they mate, their bodies can't live without it."

"They have to be bitten by their mates as often as possible, preferably no more than every couple of days, to have that additive reintroduced into their system. If they go longer than three days, a Tri Omega will start feeling weak. Four days will have them in bed. Five days could mean their life."

Serge felt a sudden foreboding. There was an undercurrent of tension in the room. Serge glanced from Siro's grim face to Niko and Vaska's hesitant-looking ones. He knew they were trying to tell him something, but he just couldn't quite figure out what they…

Serge inhaled sharply as he pressed his hand to the bite mark in his neck and then the one over his chest. He distinctly remembered Niko biting them during sex, and he remembered both men biting him when they were fighting.

"You bit me," Serge whispered. "You both bit me."

Niko and Vaska nodded, looking very nervous.

"Am I…" Serge swallowed past the lump of fear building in his throat. "Am I a Tri Omega?"

Niko and Vaska nodded again.

Serge swallowed again. "Since you both bit me, I guess that means you're my mates?"

Somehow, this time, Serge wasn't in the least bit surprised when Niko and Vaska nodded their heads. He just knew somehow. His luck seemed to be going that way. He turned to look at Siro.

"Are you my mate, too?"

Siro chuckled. "No, I'm your brother, Yurok."

Chapter 13

Vaska watched Serge pace back in forth in front of the French doors. He wasn't speaking to anyone and refused to answer even if someone asked him something. After Siro had dropped his little bomb, Serge had shut down. That had been three hours ago. Serge hadn't said a single word since. He hadn't even acknowledged that anyone else was in the room.

Vaska was really starting to get worried. He didn't know if Serge's break with reality was due to Siro's news that they were siblings, from the news that Serge was a Tri Omega, or from knowing that he was now mated to Niko and Vaska. That didn't even begin to cover that fact that Serge just found out he was a wolf.

The man had to be confused. In the last twenty-four hours his entire life had been tossed upside down. Vaska wouldn't blame Serge if he washed his hands of the whole situation. He just hoped the man didn't do that.

"Can I ask you a few questions?"

Vaska blinked for a moment, unsure if the softly spoken words had actually come from Serge until he realized the man had stopped pacing and stood facing him. He gestured for Serge to come forward. He couldn't get up. Niko was asleep between his legs with his head curled up on Vaska's lap.

"Ask me anything you like."

"Why me?"

"Why you what?"

"Why did you choose me?"

"Serge, we didn't exactly choose you." When Serge frowned, Vaska quickly went on. He didn't want the man to think they didn't want him. "We most likely would have chosen you if we had been given the chance, but fate chooses our mates for us."

"Fate?"

"We know our mates from first scent and taste. We know when we find our mates that we will be with that person for the rest of our lives. Divorce is not a word in our world. When we bite our mate, it creates a bond that can never be broken."

"Never?" Serge whispered.

Vaska shook his head.

"Tell me about this bond."

"We can talk to each other mentally," he said silently.

"Holy shit!" Serge gasped. "Can you...can you read my mind?"

"No, it doesn't work that way. We can only read the thoughts you send us."

"Us." Serge walked over and sat down in a chair by the French doors. He looked ready to fall apart. "I don't understand any of this, Vaska."

"If it makes you feel any better, we don't understand that much either. The bond between mates is sacred in our world. Mating within the wolf world is a sacred bond that overrules everything. It doesn't matter if someone mates outside of his or her immediate pack. Everyone respects the bond. The mating bond overrules everything, even the words of an alpha."

"That sounds a little intense."

Vaska chuckled. "I suppose it does, but you need to understand that the bond we have goes deeper than that between humans, much deeper. Mates can talk to each other telepathically.

We can feel our mate's emotions, know if our mate is happy or sad, upset or excited. The need to insure that our mates are happy and safe is obsessive."

"Like when I shifted and attacked Siro?"

"Exactly like that."

"Do you have any idea how crazy all of this sounds?" Serge asked as he spread his arms out. "Two days ago I knew exactly who I was. I was a hunter. I fought to save this world from wolves and now I find, not only am I one, but I'm one with special abilities and two wolf mates. Doesn't that seem odd to you?"

"Serge, six months ago I killed my brother because he was trying to kill his pregnant mate. Two days ago, I brought that baby into this world. I'll have to live the rest of my life knowing that not only did I kill my brother, but I killed that child's father. That seems odd to me." Vaska waved his hand between him, Niko, and Serge. "This thing between the three of us? That seems right to me."

"Well, sure you can say that. You've been mated to Niko for how long?"

"Four days."

Serge's moth dropped open. "You've only been mated for four days?"

"Yes, five days ago, I didn't even know Niko."

"But…" Serge frowned. "You seem so close. It's like you've been together forever."

"And I guess that is why I think we have some things easier than humans. Niko and I accept our mating because we know what it means. Discovering each other's personalities is just a bonus." When Serge opened his mouth to speak, Vaska held up his hand. "Don't get me wrong, it isn't always roses. Niko refused to accept our mating for the first two days. He didn't want a mate."

"Why?"

Vaska smiled as he looked down at Niko and gently brushed some hair back from his face. "He didn't want the responsibility I think. Niko is the beta of his pack. He's seen the worst of us and the best of us. It makes it hard for him to commit."

"He won't leave, will he?"

Vaska glanced up at Serge when he heard the worry in the man's voice. "No, not now. He's accepted us. And I think I actually have you to thank for that."

"Me?"

Vaska chuckled then gestured to the side of the bed. "Come here for a moment."

Serge looked hesitant then walked across the room to sit on the side of the bed. "What?"

"Lean down here and put your face in my neck. I want you to breathe in deeply through your nose."

"What?" Serge's eyebrows shot up in surprise.

"Just do it. I think it might help you understand."

Serge looked like he wanted to argue. His eyebrows were drawn together in a deep frown, his lips pressed together until they were almost white. But he did as Vaska directed and leaned in, pressing his face into the crook of Vaska's neck and inhaling deeply.

Vaska braced himself for what he knew was coming. Serge suddenly jerked and his body went taut. His hands gripped Vaska'a arms almost to the point of pain as he pushed his face closer to Vaska's skin, inhaling over and over again.

"You smell so fucking good," Serge groaned. "I've never smelled anything like this in my life."

A low growl filled the silence in the room. Vaska shuddered when he felt Serge's tongue stroke across his skin. Deep guttural sounds started to fill his ears as Serge climbed up on the bed and stretched out, pressing down against Vaska's side.

"You taste even better."

Vaska smiled. He had an even bigger surprise for Serge. Vaska reached down between them and pressed his hand over the impressive bulge behind Serge's zipper. Serge growled and started humping his hips against Vaska's hand.

"Oh god, yes, touch me!" Serge reached down and fumbled with his pants.

Vaska knew the man was in the midst of a mating arousal and probably didn't know what he was saying, but it was everything he could do to deny the man. He grabbed Serge's hand and held him still.

"Serge, majiktoka, you need to calm down. Sit back and take a couple of deep breaths of fresh air. You're feeling very aroused right now from smelling me. You're not in control."

"Please!"

"You go stand at the bottom of the bed, get some fresh air in your lungs and put a little distance between us. If you still want me after that, I'm all yours."

"Promise?"

Vaska groaned at the need he could see on Serge's face. He didn't want to deny his mate. But he also knew Serge wasn't in his right mind at the moment. He'd rather deny Serge now and have him be a little upset than take advantage of him and have Serge very mad at him later on.

"I promise, majiktoka."

Serge swiped his tongue across Vaska's neck one more time then backed away, moving off the bed. His half-lidded eyes watched Vaska the entire way. When he finally stood at the bottom of the bed, Serge drew in several deep breaths.

Vaska's heart fell as he watched reason slowly come back to Serge's face, his eyes clearing of the arousal and need that had filled them so much just moments before. He knew it was the right thing to do, but he wished he'd kept his mouth shut.

"What the hell just happened?" Serge asked as he pushed his hand through his hair. He looked wild-eyed, unsettled.

Vaska grimaced. "Remember we told you that we know our mates from scent?"

"Was that what that was?"

Vaska nodded.

"Holy fucking shit!" Serge gasped, sitting down on the end of the bed. "You could bottle that stuff and make millions."

"Nope." Vaska chuckled. "That scent is all ours, and we don't share."

"I'm just saying…" Serge blinked several times. "Damn. I was ready to do anything to get more. It's like a drug."

"And there is no cure."

Serge's eyes snapped up to meet Vaska's. "Exactly."

"And now you understand a little more about what it means to be mated, Serge. The scent, the sound, the sight of our mates, it's all engineered to bring us together."

"But why?" Serge glanced around for a moment, licking his lips. He looked like he was trying to organize his thoughts. "I mean, what's the point?"

"I'm not sure there is a point."

Serge suddenly jumped off the bed and started pacing again. "There has to be a point. Why are we drawn to each other like this? I can honestly say that I don't think I will ever smell something that arousing again in my life. How can that be normal?"

"You haven't smelled Niko yet."

Serge blanched. "There's two of you," he whispered.

Vaska wondered if that knowledge had just now hit Serge. "Yes, you are mated to both Niko and myself."

"Is it always going to be like this?"

"Yes, it will always be this way between us."

"How do you function? I have an uncontrollable urge to rub myself all over you. It's almost the only thing I can think about even now."

Vaska smiled. "Accepting it is half the battle, Serge. Being together is the other half." He gestured to the side of the bed again. "Come sit down and I'll show you what I mean."

Serge shook his head rapidly. "Oh, no, if I get any closer to you I don't know if I'll be able to control myself."

"Trust me, please."

Serge frowned, the corners of his lips turning down. He slowly walked over and sat down on the side of the bed, making sure that their bodies did not touch. He even leaned back a bit.

"Give me your hand." Vaska held his out, waiting for Serge to take it. The moment their skin touched, Serge heaved a deep sigh, the tension instantly draining out of his body. "See, majiktoka, isn't that better?"

"Why do I feel like I can suddenly breathe again?" Serge whispered.

"The bond between us isn't just about arousal and sex, Serge. We need each other. We need physical contact as much as possible, even if it's just holding hands." Vaska stroked his free hand down Niko's face, chuckling when the man smiled in his sleep and turned into his hand. "The simplest little touch brings us peace."

Serge swallowed hard. "And it will always be like this?"

"Yes."

"Wha-what if one of us dies?"

"We don't know what happens to a triad bonding if one of the mates does, Serge. We don't know enough about the bond a Tri Omega has with his or her mates."

"Why the hell not?"

"Throughout our history, Tri Omegas were only born one per generation, Serge. When one was born, he or she was raised by our Wolf Council so that they could develop their abilities and be a benefit to all packs. But—"

"I'm not going to any Wolf Council," Serge said as he tried to jerk his hand away from Vaska.

"No, no, majiktoka," Vaska said quickly, tightening his grip on Serge's hand. "You don't have to go anywhere. Things have changed, Serge. Now, instead of one Tri Omega being born per generation, we have an alarming number of them being born. Something is going on, and I believe that the Tri Omegas are at the heart of it."

"That means me," Serge whispered.

"It does, but I don't want you to worry about that. Niko and I won't let anything happen to you. The bond we have supersedes everything, even the wants and wishes of an alpha or the Wolf Council. We won't let anyone harm you or take you from us."

"This is all so much to take in, Vaska."

"It is, but you are not alone. You will always have me and Niko in your corner."

Serge's eyebrows drew together as he frowned again. "How can you say that? You don't even know me. I've spent my life learning how to kill wolves, not mate with one."

"And I spent my life learning how to be a doctor, not savior of Tri Omegas." Vaska leaned his head back against the pillows, wondering how much he should tell Serge. The man's feelings still weren't clear where werewolves were concerned. "I never expected to be a stop on the underground road to freedom for Tri Omegas, Serge. And yet, that's exactly what I am."

"Underground road to freedom?"

"Tri Omegas don't have an easy time of it, Serge. Many, like the little girl you met earlier, are ostracized from their packs. Some are even hunted and killed. Remember me telling you that Ana's parents were killed by the alpha of her pack? He considered her an abomination because she was a Tri Omega."

"Ana? She's just a little girl."

"And?"

"But that's…" Serge shook his head. "That's wrong."

Vaska smiled and squeezed Serge's hand. "Yes, it is, which is why instead of just being a doctor in some little country town, I am now one of the stops on the underground. I find safe places for these people to live, somewhere that no one will hurt them or try to use them for their own purposes."

"Does that happen?" Serge seemed to shiver a little.

"More than you would think." Vaska grimaced. "Suppose you were the alpha or leader of a group of people and you discovered the omega in your pack had abilities, powerful abilities, like maybe he could heal people with a touch of his hand. Wouldn't you want to be able to tap into that power?"

"I guess."

"Well, unfortunately, some alphas believe that as leaders of their packs, they have a right to tap into that power no matter what. They kill off their families and hide the Tri Omegas away in secret. They don't want to turn them over to the Wolf Council. They want to keep the Tri Omegas to themselves."

"The keep them prisoners?"

"Pretty much. Those that have escaped come here through the underground, and I find them places to stay. Others aren't as lucky."

"But…didn't Niko say he had friends that were mated to Tri Omegas?"

"Those are the lucky ones. Several of Niko's friends have ended up mated to Tri Omegas. Their mates protect them from everyone that wants to do them harm."

"Even the Wolf Council?"

"I think the Wolf Council is a little overwhelmed at the moment with the number of Tri Omegas being born. They don't know quite what to do with all of them. But you also have to remember, Niko's friends are already mated. Not even the Wolf Council can separate them from their mates."

"Then I'm safe?"

"You are to a point. Other alphas and the Wolf Council can't take you away from us. Wolf hunters can still try and kill you."

Serge sucked in a deep breath. "Christ, Vaska, what if they find Ana? I felt it was wrong to harm children and just went after the biggest and baddest wolves on our lists, but not all hunters believe that way."

"Not all hunters believe we have to be killed off either. There are groups that simply police us and only go after the wolves that go rogue. They don't hunt us just to kill us."

Vaska wondered what he said when Serge suddenly pulled his hand away, twisting it together with his other one. His head dropped down, the hair surrounding him hiding his face. "Serge?"

"Do you hate me?" Serge whispered.

"Hate you?"

"For what I was? For hunting you?"

Vaska scooted out from underneath Niko as gently as he could then moved to the side of the bed to sit next to Serge. He wrapped his arm around Serge's shoulder and grabbed his face, lifting it up to him.

"I don't hate you, Serge. I could never hate you. I disagree with what you did, but I would disagree even if you had been a wolf going after humans that you thought had wronged you. I'm a doctor. As a general rule, I don't believe in killing."

Vaska was shocked down to his toes when Serge leaned over and rested his head on Vaska's shoulder. He tightened the arm he had around Serge's shoulders and moved his hand up to stroke it through Serge's hair.

Serge seemed like a scared little boy looking for someone to care for him and protect him. It was in direct contrast to his huge body, which screamed confident warrior. Vaska's possessive streak suddenly flamed to life and grew to encompass all six-foot-six of the tall man.

"I know you're confused, Serge. I also know this is all very scary. But Niko and I will always be here for you. We take care of each other, and we protect each other. The three of us are one entity now."

"That actually sounds pretty good." Serge chuckled.

"It does. Each of us brings something different to our relationship, Serge. It makes us stronger. Apart, we are just three men. Together, we're unstoppable."

Serge leaned back, a peculiar expression on his face. "Do you think Niko feels the same way?"

Vaska opened his mouth to reply when he suddenly heard a soft chuckle from behind him. He turned to see Niko staring up at them. He turned and leaned down to give Niko a small kiss on the lips.

"Hey, majiktoka, did you have a nice nap?"

"Yeah, I guess I needed it."

"You did." Vaska stroked the back of his hand down the side of Niko's face. "You've had a pretty eventful few days."

"Why don't you let Serge in here to join us?" Niko asked through their bond.

"You two are talking, aren't you?"

Vaska glanced over his shoulder, nodding. "Yes, how did you know?"

Serge pressed a hand against his temple. "There's a buzzing in my head."

"The bond between us will get stronger with time, and you'll be able to hear better."

"I can hear the two of you talking to each other?"

Niko pushed himself up to lean on one arm. "Sure, you'll be able to hear us, and we'll be able to hear you."

"I can already hear Vaska."

Niko smiled. "You'll hear me in time, too."

"How?" Serge asked. "I mean, why can I hear Vaska but I can't hear you? Is there—"

The sound of someone knocking on the bedroom door stopped Serge from saying anything further. Vaska tensed then noticed that Serge and Niko were also tensing. He growled low in his throat and climbed to his feet. He was getting damn tired of his mates being afraid all of the time.

Vaska walked to the door and swung it open, surprised to see Markus standing there. "What?"

"Your company has arrived, Vasiliy. They are waiting downstairs in the drawing room."

"My company?"

"It's Vadim and Sasha," Niko shouted excitedly.

Vaska turned and watched his mate hop off the bed and race across the floor. He grabbed Niko right before he would have dashed out the door. "Whoa, slow down, Niko. We don't know for sure that it's Vadim and Sasha."

"Who else could it be?"

"Nikolai is correct, Vasiliy, Alpha Miroslav and his mate, Sashenka, have arrived."

"Alpha Vadim Mirolsav?"

Vaska frowned and glanced over at Serge, concerned by the slight horror he could hear in the man's voice and even more alarmed by the paleness of his face. "Yes, Vadim is Niko's brother. Why?"

"Vaska." Serge swallowed hard, looking worse by the second. "Vadim Miroslav is higher up on the hunter's kill list than you. He's considered a *kill on sight* wolf. The hunter that kills him would be one of the highest ranked hunters in the world."

"Do you plan on killing him?"

Serge paled even more. "How can you ask me that?"

"Well, you seemed to be obsessed with how far Vadim is up on the hunter's list. What do you want me to think?"

"I want you to think that I'm trying to protect you. If Vadim Miroslav is here then the hunters aren't far behind." Serge's hands moved through the air as if he was greatly agitated. "How in the hell do you think I found you so easily?"

Vaska frowned. "How did you find me?"

"Someone called me and gave me your direct location. He gave me directions, the code to the back door. He even told me where the secret entrance to the basement was located and told me that there were a bunch of wolves down there. He told me everything about you." Serge pointed to Niko. "He even told me about Niko."

"He?" Vaska asked. He stiffened, his body going rigid as if bracing for something horrific. "He who?"

Chapter 14

Niko could see the storm that was brewing between Serge and Vaska. Both men were stubborn, and both men needed to be smacked over the head. They were fighting each other when they should have been fighting whatever adversary they faced.

"All right!" Niko shouted through their bond as loud as he could. *"That's enough out of both of you!"*

Vaska blinked.

Serge grabbed the side of his head, wobbled a little, then sat down on the side of the bed. "Well, I heard that."

Niko smirked and crossed his arms over his chest. "Unless either of you want to find out what being without a mate is really like, I suggest that you make up and start working together, because you're creating more problems than you are solving."

"Niko—"

Niko waved his hand through the air, stopping Vaska. "No, we're supposed to be a team, all three of us. And yet, the two of you keep going at each other's throats almost every time you open your mouths. I've had enough."

Niko wasn't sure what he expected when he basically laid down the law to Serge and Vaska, but it wasn't the deep chuckle and grin that came his way from both men.

"Is he always this assertive?" Serge asked.

"Got me, we haven't known each other that long." Vaska clasped his hands together in front of him and bounced back on the heels of his feet. "But it's kind of hot."

Niko turned to glare at Markus when the man laughed. "You have something to add to the conversation?"

The smile quickly fell from Markus's face. "Nope, not a thing. I'll just go downstairs and make refreshments for everyone, make sure your guests are comfortable."

"You do that."

Markus turned and hurried away.

"Niko!" Vaska admonished. "Be nice to Markus."

Niko rolled his eyes then turned to look back at Serge. "Are you going to tell Vaska who gave you your information?"

"I don't know his name. He called and gave me the information then hung up."

"And you believed him?" Vaska asked.

"Of course not," Serge scoffed. "This wasn't my first hunt. I had been watching Vaska. I saw the two of you walking together in the fog. After I attacked Niko on the street, I was pretty injured. I went back to my hotel room to rest up when this man called. I came out here and watched the place until I spotted you two through the windows. I knew at least some of the information the man gave me was right."

"Okay, so someone is obviously trying to get Vaska killed," Niko said. "I nominate Andrei for scum of the earth."

"Andrei?" Vaska said. "If he wanted to kill me, why not just do it? Why try and take everyone else down with me?"

Niko shrugged. "Why think he could give me a better time than you?"

"He what?" Serge snapped.

"Andrei seemed to think he could show me a good time. A few nights ago he was waiting for me in my room, naked on my bed. He offered to let me fuck him."

Serge growled. Claws extended out of his fingertips. "He damn well better keep his naked ass away from you, or I'll rip him a new one."

Niko arched an eyebrow and sauntered across the room to stand in front of Serge. He stroked his hand down Serge's firm muscular chest. "Are you going to give me something else to fuck?"

Serge grabbed Niko's arms. "I can do better than that," he growled. "I can fuck you until you never think about another man again."

"What about Vaska?"

"He can fuck you, too." Desire started burning in Serge's milky blue eyes. "You won't even have the energy to think of other men."

Niko opened his mouth to point out that he hadn't been thinking of other men. Andrei had just showed up naked in his bed. And then Niko felt Vaska press up against him from behind. Niko swallowed quickly instead of speaking. He doubted he would have been able to form a single word anyway. Vaska and Serge had started rubbing their hands over Niko's body.

Niko was all for both men fucking him. He just wanted to be able to do a little fucking back. He had no intention of being the bottom boy for both men for the rest of his life. He'd already been inside Serge's ass. He just had to get inside Vaska's ass.

"How about you fuck me and I fuck Vaska?"

Serge shook his head. "Uh uh, we're going to take turns fucking you this time. You can fuck Vaska next time."

"What about our guests?" Niko asked.

Serge smirked. "Markus can take care of them for a little while."

Niko was ecstatic about Serge's new assertiveness and acceptance of their relationship. He just wondered how long it was going to last. Vaska seemed to be totally onboard with their mating. Serge seemed to wobble back and forth, one minute being totally for it, the next minute not sure how he felt. This was so much better.

"Strip."

Niko arched his eyebrow again. "Make me."

Serge held up his hand and flicked out a claw. Niko swallowed hard as the man started slicing his clothes off. Serge was learning fast.

He was going to have this wolf thing down to an art form in no time at all.

Vaska started slicing Niko's clothes off from behind. Niko didn't dare breathe until the last item of cut-up clothing fell to the floor. He might end up with something vital getting chopped off and wouldn't that be a sad state of affairs.

Niko looked down at himself, smirking when he noted his cock arched up to his abdomen. He looked back up at Serge. "So, I'm naked, so what?"

Niko yelped a moment later as he flew through the air and landed on the bed, bouncing several times. He started to quickly turn over when twin weights settled down on either side of him, holding his body down to the mattress.

"Okay." Niko chuckled nervously. "I was just joking guys."

"We weren't, majiktoka," Vaska growled into his ear. "By the time we're done with you, you won't have the brain capacity to form a complete sentence."

"Vaska, really, we can just—" Niko inhaled sharply when he felt two lubed fingers push into his ass. He hadn't been expecting it and the burn was intense. He hadn't even heard someone get the lube. "Wha-what are you doing?"

"Serge's just getting you ready, majiktoka."

"Ready?" Niko started panting as Serge's fingers moved swiftly in and out of him.

"Once Serge has you all primed and ready to go, you're going to sit on his cock while we have a little fun."

"Fun?" Niko chocked out.

His mind was starting to melt, but he could have sworn Vaska said he was going to sit on Serge's cock *while* he and Vaska had fun. What kind of fun could the two of them have while he was impaled on Serge's cock?

Niko barely had time to adjust to the two fingers in his ass before a third one was added, then a fourth. He really hadn't gotten a lot of time to look at Serge, but just how many damn fingers did the man need?

As full as he felt and as much as it burned, Niko still groaned in protest when Serge pulled his fingers away. He much preferred being full than empty, even if it was just by his mate's fingers.

"Serge, please," Niko groaned. His skin felt hot like it was about to burn right off of his body. He knew if Vaska or Serge would just touch him, he would feel so much better.

"Please what, Niko?"

"I'm so empty." He ached to be filled.

"I think I can fix that, Niko."

Niko's yelp of surprise turned into a long drawn-out groan as Serge's cock filled him from behind. As Serge thrust in until he hit bottom, Niko suddenly understood why the man had used four fingers to stretch him out. Serge was massive.

"Move," Niko demanded, his hands gripping the blankets tightly.

Instead of moving like Niko wanted, Serge grabbed him around the waist and hauled him back against his chest. Niko cried out as he sank a little further down Serge's cock. He didn't know there was any room left in his ass, but apparently there was.

"Now the fun begins," Vaska said as he scooted forward to kneel in front of Niko.

Niko had no idea what Vaska had planned. His ass was already occupied with Serge's cock. His legs were spread wide as he straddled Serge's thick thighs. Niko's hands gripped Serge's arms where they wrapped around his stomach.

When Vaska leaned toward him, Niko reached out and tried to grab him. He wanted one mate plastered against his back and the other plastered against his front. But Vaska quickly moved out of his reach and wagged a finger back and forth in front of him.

"Uh uh, majiktoka, no touching."

"No touching?" Niko whispered the words with horror.

"In fact, I think you should wrap your arms around Serge's neck."

Niko blinked then slowly raised his arms and wrapped them around Serge's neck, clasping them behind Serge's head. He watched Vaska move toward him again. His breath caught in his throat as anticipation filled him.

Vaska seemed to be moving at a snail's pace. Niko wanted to scream in frustration as he watched Vaska's finger slowly rise into the air and reach out toward his nipple. By the time Vaska's fingertips grazed his nipple, Niko was so primed he cried out and arched into the air as the small touch sent electricity flaring through him.

It was just one small touch, and Niko couldn't seem to catch his breath. When Vaska moved to the other nipple, flicking his finger over the taut little nub, Niko thought he was going to lose his mind. Each flick of Vaska's finger, each tug, seemed to send sensations exploding through his body.

"Vaska, please." Niko knew he was begging. He just didn't care. He ached. He needed. He…oh damn, Serge kept his arousal in a fever pitch by moving Niko up and down on his cock every few moments. Niko never had a chance to take in a breath.

Niko shuddered when Vaska leaned in and stroked his tongue across Niko's sensitive nipple. The man seemed to enjoy alternating between Niko's two nipples, sometimes licking, other times gently tugging with his teeth. Both were driving Niko crazy. There seemed to be a direct connection from Niko's nipples to his cock.

When Vaska moved down his chest, licking every inch, Niko didn't think he would be able to stand it. His cock ached so much it almost hurt. Serge wasn't helping matters in the least. His small little thrusts had worked into more forceful ones, each one driving his cock deep into Niko's ass.

When Vaska's tongue flickered over the head of Niko's cock, he was done for. Niko cried out as an intense bone-shaking orgasm swept over him. As he slumped back against Serge, Niko didn't even have the energy to feel embarrassed that he had shot all over Vaska's face.

When Vaska moved out of the way, lying on his back, Niko just watched. He was too melty to do anything else. He could feel his cock try to take interest when Vaska grabbed his own cock and began stroking it. It throbbed and pulsed a couple of times. Niko just didn't think he had the energy to do anything about it.

Serge suddenly pushed him forward and started thrusting into him. Niko laid his head down on Vaska's thigh, his eyes mesmerized by the movement of the man's hand as it went up and down. Vaska's hand was tanned, but his cock, fully engorged, was darker. The contrast of colors really was a lovely sight.

Niko reached and gently cupped Vaska's balls. The lightly furred little sac instantly drew up close to Vaska's body and a long groan fell from the man. Niko grinned and stroked his fingertips over the tight ball sac.

"You'd better hurry, Serge," Vaska snapped. "I'm either coming in Niko's ass or I'm coming in your ass, but I'm coming soon."

Niko grunted and pushed his hands into the mattress to hold his position when Serge suddenly started pounding into him at a breakneck speed. If Niko didn't know better, he would have thought that fucking was Serge's Tri Omega ability. The man was very good at it.

Niko could even feel his cock taking a renewed interest in what was happening. He could feel his cock start to fill again, harden, and bounce with the force of Serge's thrusts.

He ached to grab his cock and stroke himself off as Vaska was doing, but Serge's rammed into him so powerfully that Niko knew he would have been pushed up the bed if he did. He could only kneel there and take it. It wasn't a bad way to go really, just frustrating.

Serge suddenly stiffened behind him. Niko jerked as a loud roar filled the room even as Serge's hot seed filled his ass. He hadn't expected Serge to make such a deep feral noise. He was even less prepared for the sharp canine teeth that sank into his shoulder a moment later.

Niko felt something deep inside of him suddenly snap into place and cried out. It was a small feeling that grew with each suck of blood that Serge drew in until it exploded, drowning Niko in light.

He could feel everything Serge felt, all the longing, the need, even the fear of being mated. Everything Serge felt was coming through loud and clear. Niko almost turned and drew the man into his arms. Sex was a great way to communicate, but it wasn't the only way. Niko would have to show Serge the others ways, and maybe Vaska too.

Serge's canine's abruptly pulled free of Niko's neck. Niko cried out in protest as Serge pulled away from him. He wondered if he had done something wrong until Serge lifted him up and placed him over the top of Vaska.

Niko's head rolled back on his shoulders as he was gently lowered down onto Vaska's cock. Serge stayed behind him, the man's body propping him up as Vaska grabbed Niko's hips and started thrusting up into him.

Niko had no idea when they said that they were both going to fuck him that they really meant it. He'd have to remember to take them at their word next time, or beg. Niko felt like a rag doll or a sex toy, either description fit his circumstances at the moment.

His body was being used for his mates' pleasure, and he couldn't be happier about it. If they wanted to play *man in the middle* again, Niko would be the first to volunteer. He was in heaven, sensation after exquisite sensation racing through his body.

"My turn, majiktoka." Vaska gestured with his finger for Niko to come closer.

Niko flopped down over the top of Vaska. His eyes rolled back in his head when Vaska's teeth sank into the soft flesh between his neck and shoulder on the opposite side from Serge. He was now marked by both his mates, bonded to both of them.

Niko's vision started to blur, so he just closed his eyes. He could feel his mates through their mutual bond anyway. Vaska was getting ready to come and Serge was gearing up for another round.

Niko groaned as his ass was assaulted over and over again, Vaska's thrusts becoming wild and erratic. The moment Vaska retracted his teeth and leaned back, Niko struck, sinking his own canines into the soft flesh of the man's neck.

Vaska grunted loudly. His hands tightened on Niko's hips as he filled Niko's ass with his release. Niko groaned as Vaska's body started to settle. He was so hard he felt like his dick was about to crack in two. He needed to come.

Niko started to push himself up off of Vaska so he could grab his cock when he was suddenly lifted all of the way off. Before he could ask Serge what he was doing, Niko felt the man's cock sink back into him.

Niko was a little more sensitive this time and winced when Serge filled him completely. He didn't have more than a second to wait before the man was once again pounding into him. There was no soft build up this time.

However, the fucking he was getting this time did include a hand wrapped around his cock. Niko groaned and leaned back against Serge's larger body. He opened his eyes and looked down only to find Vaska watching him, his eyes intense and filled with waning desire.

"Come for Serge, majiktoka," Vaska ordered. "Come on his cock."

Vaska's sexy words had their desired effect on Niko. He started panting heavily. He could feel his orgasm building at an alarming rate and knew this one would be so intense he might pass out.

"Come on, majiktoka, show us how much you want us."

Niko couldn't hold himself up any longer. His bones were melting right along with his brain. He fell forward, landing on his hands. He felt like collapsing further down onto his stomach, but Vaska had a hold of his cock, and he wasn't going to give that up unless forced to.

"Fuck him, Serge, fuck him hard," Vaska said. "Give him every last inch of that beautiful cock of yours."

Niko almost lost his grip on the blankets when Serge's thrusts suddenly increased in speed and strength. The sudden swelling of Serge's cock inside of him combined with the loud roar that filled the room sent Niko over the edge.

Vaska's grip tightened around his aching erection. Niko's body overloaded, sensations racing through him like a rocket. He cried out and came all over Vaska's hand just as Serge came inside of him.

This time, Niko couldn't keep his body from collapsing down on top of Vaska. He rested his head against Vaska's heart, the steady thump beneath his ear bringing a sense of peace to Niko he hadn't felt in a very long time. He could feel Serge's larger body blanketing him from behind. He was surrounded by his mates. It was heaven.

"How are you doing, majiktoka?" Vaska asked as he stroked his fingers through Niko's sweat-soaked hair.

"Hmmm."

Vaska chuckled. "I told you that you wouldn't be able to form a complete sentence."

Chapter 15

Serge shook his head as he followed Niko and Vaska down the stairs. The two men were arguing over who made whom mindless with passion. Personally, Serge thought he'd done a pretty good job himself.

He might not have been able to fuck Vaska, yet, but he'd done a damn good job of fucking Niko twice. He couldn't wait until he had a chance to go at Vaska. Just the image alone had enough power to make Serge groan and adjust himself.

When he looked up, Niko was smirking at him. Serge merely arched an eyebrow and thrust his hips forward in a clear invitation. Niko's face flushed, and he quickly looked away, hurrying the rest of the way down the stairs.

Serge chuckled and followed. The closer to the drawing that they got and the more nervous Serge grew. He was about to meet Alpha Vadim Miroslav and his mate. Both men were legends in the hunter world, Vadim a little more so than Sashenka. He was the alpha after all.

He wanted Niko's family to accept him. He didn't expect that it would happen though. He was a wolf hunter. He knew what that meant. The likelihood of Niko's family accepting him after they learned what he had been was close to nothing.

Serge was amazed at how much his life had changed in a matter of days. If someone had told him a week ago that he would feel desperate to have a bunch of wolves accept him, he would have punched them right in the mouth.

And yet, here he was, following his two mates into the drawing room to meet one of the most feared alpha's known to the hunters, and hoping that said alpha accepted him instead of ripping his throat out. He was doomed.

Serge paused at the entrance to the drawing room and glanced around. The first thing he learned as a hunter was to always be cautious and to always get the lay of the land before entering any room. He didn't think that behavior was going to change now that he was no longer a hunter. There were some things that were just too ingrained to end.

Besides, it was better for his health if the look on the large man standing by the fireplace was anything to go by. Alpha Miroslav had spotted him, and the man did not look happy. His forehead wrinkled as his eyebrows furrowed together. There was even a slight curling at the corner of his mouth. Serge was surprised there wasn't a growl.

Vadim Miroslav may have looked casual to everyone else as he moved forward and placed himself between Serge and the small man at his side, but Serge wasn't fooled. The alpha was placing himself between his mate and the danger he saw in Serge.

Vaska and Niko seemed to be oblivious to what was happening between Vadim and Serge. Niko was talking animatedly as he gestured to Vaska then Serge. He had a huge smile on his face as he talked to the alpha's mate. Vaska just seemed to stand there, hanging on Niko's every word.

Serge was pretty sure neither man had clued in to the tension growing in the room. Serge could feel it though, and he almost choked on it. He could feel his canines wanting to drop down and rubbed his tongue over his gums as he tried to steady his breathing.

His body was starting to react to the danger it sensed. Serge had had that happen before. He just never shifted before. Usually, his body tensed as if readying for a fight. This time, his body tensed, but Serge could feel the wolf moving right under his skin, wanting out.

Serge hadn't been shifting for more than a few hours at most. He'd actually only done it once. He didn't know how to control it, and he was terrified that his wolf would take over and come out, maybe attack someone.

"Vaska!" he whispered through their bond, hoping that the man would hear him.

Vaska's head whipped around instantly, concern filling his deep blue eyes. Serge saw his eyes widen and then the man hurried across the room to him. Serge leaned into the hands that rubbed up and down his arms, feeling his wolf retreat.

He heaved a sigh of relief when he felt his control reassert itself and could finally unclench his fists. It amazed him that the simple touch of his mate's hands could calm him so quickly, but he wasn't going to question it. He was going to grab onto it, and Vaska, and not let them go. It seemed to be the only way to keep his wolf at bay.

"Are you okay?"

Serge nodded. "I'm getting there."

"What happened?"

"He happened." Serge gestured toward Alpha Miroslav.

"Vadim?" Vaska glanced over his shoulder at the alpha.

"Yeah."

"Serge, you haven't even met him yet. Don't buy trouble. It's going to be okay."

"I may not have met him, but he's been speaking volumes since I walked into the room."

Serge saw the frown wrinkle Vaska's face and wondered if his mate believed him. Vaska certainly didn't have any reason to. Serge hadn't proved that he was trustworthy to anyone, let alone his mates. For all they knew, he could still be in hunter mode.

"Do you want me to ask him to leave?"

"What?" Surely Serge couldn't have heard Vaska right. His mate was offering to make an alpha leave because he was feeling a little uncomfortable? Serge grinned as a sudden unfamiliar calm over came him. "No, but thank you for offering. I guess I just need to get used to being on the other side of things."

"Are you ready to meet Vadim and Sasha?"

Serge eyed the large alpha carefully. "Is he going to eat me?"

"Um, I don't think so, but I can always ask."

Serge glanced over at Vaska as they started walking across the room. He chuckled when he found the man smiling back at him. "Come on, I guess we'd better get this over with."

"Serge, you're not walking to your doom."

"Says you." Serge gestured to Vadim. "Have you seen how he's looking at me? He's waiting for the first sign of me being a hunter, and then he's going to attack. I don't know enough about this shifting thing to fight him properly."

Vaska suddenly turned and grabbed both of Serge's arms. "Serge, he's not waiting for you to turn into a hunter. He's protecting his mate just like you did with me and Siro. Vadim has never met you, and he's just doing what comes naturally to any mated wolf."

"He looks like he's going to rip my throat out."

"And he probably will if you make a move toward his mate. Not only is Vadim a mated wolf, he's also the alpha of his pack." Vaska leaned closer as if he had a big secret to share. "That's like a double whammy in the wolf world."

Serge arched an eyebrow, amused at Vadim's choice of words—a double whammy. What exactly did that mean? Before Serge could ask Vaska about the strange phrase, they were suddenly standing right in front of Alpha Vadim Miroslav.

"Alpha Miroslav," Serge said.

"Serge Dmitriev," the man said slowly. "I've heard of you."

"I've heard of you, too."

"You have quite the reputation for hunting and killing my kind." Vadim glanced around at the others in the room before coming back to Serge. "Which begs the question, why are you here?"

"Things aren't always what they seem."

Vadim arched one eyebrow, his head tilting slightly in a curious motion. "Are you saying you haven't made it your mission in life to wipe wolves off the face of the earth?"

"Like I said, things aren't always what they seem, alpha. Things change."

"Not that much they don't," Vadim snorted.

"They do when you find yourself a mated Tri Omega." Serge had the pleasure of watching Vadim's mouth drop open in shock. He even saw Sasha's surprised face peek out from behind the man.

"You're a Tri Omega?" Vadim asked.

"It would seem so, yes."

"Prove it."

Serge rolled his eyes and reached for the buttons on his shirt. A sudden low growl froze him where he was. He didn't even have to turn his head to look. He knew that growl anywhere. Niko was livid.

Serge reached and grabbed Niko's arm just as the man started to step past him. "Niko, baby, stop. Your brother has every right to question me. I was a hunter, and I did make it my mission in life to hunt and kill wolves."

Niko's head whipped around. His eyes narrowed and started to go lupine black. "He doesn't have the right to see you naked."

"How else is he going to know if I can shift?"

"Find another way," Niko snapped. "He doesn't get to see you naked. Only Vaska and I do."

"Fuck me running," Vadim said. "You're mated to Vaska and Niko."

"Yes," Serge answered, wondering how Vadim would take the news. As Vadim was the brother of Niko, they had a family bond that would always be in place. Nothing barring death would ever change it. With the strange way Vadim was staring at him, Serge had to wonder if the man planned on severing that tie through his death.

"Well, I guess that kind of changes things, doesn't it?"

Serge blinked. Those weren't the words he was expecting.

"Welcome to the family, Serge."

Serge felt like he was floating in a dream world as he shook the hand that Vadim held out to him. He couldn't understand why Vadim suddenly accepted him when a moment ago, the man had been ready to kill him. He had to know.

"Why?"

Vadim smirked as he wrapped his arm around his mate's shoulders and pulled the little man forward to stand at his side. "You've mated Niko."

"And?"

"And, Niko would never do anything to endanger Sasha. If Niko accepts you as his mate, and I can see by his actions that he does, then I have to also."

"You do remember that I am a wolf hunter, right?"

"You *were* a wolf hunter," Vadim said. "Now you're a mated Tri Omega. That makes all the difference in the world."

"How can you be so sure that I won't still try to kill you?" Serge asked. "You are higher up on the hunter kill list than almost anyone. I could build my reputation on your hide alone."

"Serge!" both Vaska and Niko snapped at the same time.

"Because if you hurt me, you'd hurt Niko, and you can't do that. It would be like chewing off your own arm." Vadim just chuckled. "Why do you think you're still standing there in one piece? If it wasn't for Niko, I would have killed you by now."

"You could have tried." Serge chuckled. He felt his muscles start to loosen, the tension slowly draining from his body. He was starting to like the big alpha. Vadim had a wicked sense of humor that Serge could relate to.

Serge took a step back and arched his eyebrow when the little man beside Vadim started bouncing in place, yanking on Vadim's shirt. He looked like a bundle of energy. Serge was suddenly thankful that his mates were big strong men. He didn't think he could handle a little guy like Sasha.

"Vadi!"

"Sorry, majiktoka," Vadim said. "Serge, I'd like you to meet my mate, Sasha."

Serge nodded, but made sure he didn't make any moves toward the man. He wasn't stupid. Vadim would kill him in a second if he thought Serge was the mildest of threats toward his mate. Serge would have done the same.

"It's very nice to finally meet you, Sasha. I've heard a lot about you."

"Me?" Sasha beamed. "Did you hear that, Vadi? He's heard about me."

"Majiktoka, I don't think he meant that in a good way. If he's heard about you then it means you're on the hunter's hit list with me." A muscle ticked in Vadim's jaw. "Isn't that right, Serge?"

"Unfortunately, it is. Sasha isn't as high on the list as you are, but he is on it. Most of us have heard of your mating and know that taking Sasha out is the quickest way to incapacitate you."

"It would," Vadim answered.

Serge admired the man's honesty. He was just surprised by it.

"Crap!" Sasha groaned. "That means you just upped my security, doesn't it?"

"Yep."

"Damn!"

Serge chuckled. The two men were cute together, although he'd never tell them that. He liked breathing. Serge turned and smiled over at Niko when he felt the man's arm wrap around him.

"Hey, babe."

"They're cute, aren't they?"

"Ssshhh." Serge held his finger up to his mouth. "You probably don't want to say that to them."

"Oh please, I've said worse."

"He has." Vadim chuckled, making Serge aware that the man heard their conversation. "Niko used to go on and on about how he never wanted to be mated because he didn't want the responsibility. Guess karma has a sense of humor after all, because that certainly seemed to come around and bite him in the ass."

"Vik is going to fall over laughing on this one," Sasha said. "I can't wait to tell him."

"Oh now—" Niko started only to be cut off by the loud alarm that suddenly started blaring. He jumped and swung around.

"Oh shit"—Vaska gasped—"not again."

Serge's eyes widened as Vaska ran from the room. Niko raced over to the windows and looked out. His face was pale when he turned back.

"Niko?"

"I'm going to need your help."

"You have it," Serge replied. "Anything."

"That was the perimeter alarm, which means someone is coming. We need to protect the people downstairs."

"Ana?"

Niko nodded. "And a few others."

Serge started to hurry over to Niko when his head suddenly went blank then filled with a bright white light. He stumbled to a stop. All sounds around him faded away. His eyesight dulled then blanked out all together. Even the scents in the room drifted away until he smelled nothing. It was like being inside of a bubble where nothing got inside.

But slowly, Serge began to see things. It started with his sense of smell first, and it was slow in coming. Little by little, whatever he smelled became stronger as if it were coming closer. Then Serge's sight came back, fading back in from the sides of his eyes until a complete picture was formed.

Serge still couldn't understand what he was seeing until the buzzing he heard in his head turned into sounds he could recognize. He tried to put all of the pieces of the puzzle together, and when he did, his blood ran cold.

A group of men were headed in their direction. There had to be at least ten of them, all heavily armed and dressed in black clothing. Serge knew from experience that they were dressed in black so that they would blend in with the darkness. He'd been dressed just the same more times than he could count.

Unfortunately, he also knew what that meant. They were under attack, and the people coming didn't plan on leaving anyone behind alive. Serge knew that beyond a doubt. He just wasn't sure what to do about it.

He blinked rapidly and grabbed for the nearest strong surface as his head suddenly cleared. He ended up grabbing onto Niko.

"Serge, are you okay?"

Serge winced when he shook his head. The pain pounding through his brain right now made it nearly impossible to form a coherent thought. Knowing the effect his mate had on him, Serge pushed closer to Niko and grabbed the man's hand, pressing it against the side of his head.

"Serge?"

"They're coming, about ten men all dressed in black and very heavily armed. They know we're here, all of us, and they plan to kill every last one of us, even Ana." Serge cringed as he gave everyone that bit of news. He was intrigued with Ana because she seemed to have no fear of him at all, unlike a lot of people.

"They know about Ana?"

Serge carefully nodded then allowed Niko to pull his hand away when he didn't feel any more pain. "They know about Ana and Uri and everyone else in the basement. They also know how to get down there."

"Oh, Vaska isn't going to like this," Niko whispered.

"Who are Ana and Uri?" Vadim asked.

Serge turned to face the man. He had almost forgotten Vadim and Sasha were still in the room. He quickly glanced at Niko. "He doesn't know?"

"There hasn't been time to tell him yet."

"Niko, we don't have time now." Serge pointed to the window. "Those men are coming and they are coming now. We have about twenty minutes if we're lucky."

"Then I suggest we get our asses downstairs and see what we can do."

Serge nodded and started across the room. He'd made it about halfway when Vaska came running back into the room. His face was flushed red, his hands clenched at his sides. Serge could feel the waves of rage rolling off of his mate and took a step back. He hadn't seen Vaska that angry since they fought each other.

"Vaska?"

"That damn Andrei is leading them right to us."

"Andrei!" Niko snapped.

Serge swung around to stare at Niko, noting how angry the man looked, then turned back to Vaska. "Who is Andrei?"

"Andrei used to be my brother's beta. Niko and I suspect he was also my brother's mate as well as Juliette's."

"Juliette?"

"Uri's mother."

"Oh."

"Who is Uri?" Vadim snapped.

"My nephew," Vaska answered. "I killed my brother, Ivan, six months ago. Uri was born a couple of days ago."

"Who are all of these people?" Vadim asked as he spread his arms wide.

"Tri Omegas."

Serge imagined his face looked as surprised as Vadim's when he found out about being a Tri Omega. The man looked stunned.

"Just how many do you have?"

"Including Serge, eleven or so, but you never know when another one might show up. It happens a lot."

"You have eleven Tri Omegas here in this house?" Vadim snapped. "Right now?"

"It's a long story, Vad," Niko said, "and we'll explain it all when there aren't a band of hunters coming after us. Right now, we need to get everyone to safety. If Andrei is leading these guys in, I suspect that they will head right for the basement."

"And just where in the hell are we supposed to take them, Niko?"

Serge knew from the sudden tensing of Vadim's body that he knew what Niko was going to say and he didn't like it. He turned to look at Niko and was a little surprised by the grin that appeared on Niko's face.

"Vourdala Island," Niko said, "where else?"

Chapter 16

Niko rubbed his hands together to keep them from shaking as he watched everyone running around packing down in the basement. He knew the plan was a good one, but he still didn't like it. He didn't want to be separated from his mate no matter how much it was needed.

"There has to be another way," Vaska whispered.

"Vaska," Niko said as he grabbed his mate's face in his hands. "I don't like it anymore than you do, but this is the only way. You and Vadim need to get everyone to safety while Serge and I stay here and keep the hunters busy."

"Why don't you go? I can stay here and keep the hunters busy."

"Vaska, you're a doctor, and you are also the one that these people depend on and feel safe with. They need you."

"I need you."

Niko smiled. "I need you, too."

He turned his head and looked around until he spotted Serge standing in the corner holding Ana in his arms. Her brother stood beside him holding Serge's hand. Neither of the children looked like they planned on going anywhere anytime soon. And Serge looked like he was happy as a clam right where he was.

Interesting.

"Serge, can you come over here for a moment?" Niko asked through their bond. *"Vaska needs us at the moment."*

Niko couldn't help but smile when Serge set Ana on her feet then squatted down in front of both the small children. Niko had no idea what Serge said to the two children, but it was enough to get Ana to take her thumb out of her mouth and say something back.

A moment later, the thumb was back in and Ana was nodding her head. Serge patted both children on the top of their heads then stood up and walked over. He looked tense, but there was a spark of calm in his eyes that Niko found intriguing.

"What?" Niko asked the moment Serge stopped beside him.

Serge arched an eyebrow.

Niko gestured to the two children. "What was that all about?"

Serge glanced over his shoulder. When Ana smiled and waved, Serge waved back. He had a ghost of a smile on his face when he turned back. "Ana and Timothy were a little scared. I told them that there was nothing to be afraid of."

"And?" Niko knew there was an *and*.

Serge flushed and glanced away. "And they could stay with us when we got to Vourdala Island."

"You want Ana and Timothy to stay with us?"

"They don't have anyone," Serge replied. "They need us."

Niko opened his mouth to protest until he saw the glint of uncertainty in Serge's eyes. He realized that this was something Serge really wanted, but he was bracing himself to be told no. Niko didn't have the heart to do it.

Niko sighed. "Well, I guess we will have to make some sort of arrangements then. Right now, I have a suite in Vadim's alpha compound. I think we need our own house if these two kids are going to come live with us."

Serge's smile was slow in coming, almost as if he didn't quite believe the words he was hearing, but it did come. "Yeah? We can keep them?"

"We can as long as Vadim approves it," Niko said. "Once we arrive at Vourdala Island, Vadim will be the alpha. He has final say on things like this."

"What about the Wolf Council?" Vaska asked. "If they usually take the Tri Omegas and raise them, how can Vadim go against them?"

Niko frowned. He hadn't thought of that. He planted one hand on his hip and rubbed his chin with the other one. There had to be a way that they could keep Ana and Timothy if that's what everyone agreed on.

"Vadim?" Niko finally called out. "Can I talk with you for a moment?"

Niko prayed that his brother would have an idea about what to do with Ana and Timothy. He would hate to break Serge's heart. The man seemed to want the two small Tri Omegas very much. Niko was kind of amazed. He never knew Serge had such a soft streak in him.

"What's up?"

"Ana and Timothy have no family. Their parents were killed when their alpha tried to take them. We'd like to keep them with us when we get to Vourdala Island. Is there a way to make that happen?"

Vadim glanced over his shoulder to the two small children standing in the corner. "Their parents were killed?"

"Yes."

Vadim grimaced as he turned back. "Do they have any other family?"

"I imagine they do, but they cannot be returned to their pack. Their alpha is either trying to keep them prisoner for his own purposes or kill them."

"What do they want?"

"I don't know, but they seem to have formed a bond with Serge."

Vaska snickered. "You mean Ana decided she wanted Serge and that's the end of it."

"Yeah, pretty much." Niko chuckled.

Vadim looked confused.

"Ana may be a four-year-old little girl, but she's a force to be reckoned with. Whatever you do, don't get the girl upset. She'll make your ears bleed." Niko shook his head as he looked at the innocent-looking little girl. "I'd rather face the hunters with my arms tied behind my back."

"That little girl?" Vadim pointed.

"Yeah, *that* little girl."

"And you still want her to come live with you?"

Niko shrugged. "Call us glutton for punishment. Still, Ana and Timothy need a family."

"Well, I don't know what would happen as they are both Tri Omegas, but orphaned children have been bonded with new families. All you need is a simple blood exchange. A finger prick would work."

"And that would insure that we get to keep them?"

"The Wolf Council can't take children away from bonded families."

Niko grabbed Serge's arm when the man started toward the children. "Serge, honey, you need to ask Ana and Timothy if this is what they want before we do it. Once we bond with them, it can't be changed."

Serge looked like he wanted to argue. His forehead furrowed for a moment, and then he nodded. "I know, I just—"

"She got to you, didn't she?"

"They both did." Serge sighed and glanced over at the children. "They're so small and so innocent. Their entire lives have been destroyed because of people like me."

"Serge."

Serge's eyes were filled with agony as he turned to look at Niko. "How am I supposed to fix that? How can I even expect them to look at me without hatred?"

"You didn't hurt them, Serge. Their alpha did," Niko said quickly. "They have more reason to be afraid of Vadim than they do you."

Niko ignored the small snort that came from his brother and cupped Serge's face in his hands. "Honey, you didn't do this."

"No, but I've done a lot of other bad things."

"And now you're going to do a lot of good things." Niko pointed to Ana and Timothy. "And we can start with providing a good family for them, a place where they are safe and loved. Isn't that better?"

Serge nodded. "Yeah, but—"

"No buts, Serge," Vaska said as he stepped up to them. "Go ask Ana and Timothy what they want. If they agree to be part of our family, then fine. If not, we'll find them another family to live with. It has to be their choice."

Serge didn't say anything as he pulled away and walked across the room, but Niko could see the struggle he was having with himself. He could feel the apprehension through their mating bond.

Niko clenched his fists and turned away. "I hate this."

"I know, majiktoka, but we can't force Ana and Timothy to stay with us."

"Oh, I know that." Niko waved Vaska's words away. "I'm talking about Serge being so hard on himself. His family was killed when he was five years old. He saw what he did through five-year-old eyes. How was he supposed to know wolves didn't kill his family?"

"What's this?" Vadim asked. "Did wolves kill Serge's family or hunters?"

"We don't know. It could have been wolves, but we think it was hunters and that they came back and took Serge, telling him that wolves killed them. They raised him to hate wolves, to hunt them." Niko waved back over his shoulder. "That's why he did what he did. He saw his family die and was brought up believing wolves did it."

"I think it's understandable then that he did what he did," Vadim said.

"You believe that, and I believe that," Niko said, "but I don't think he does. Serge's going to beat himself up for quite a long time over what he's done in the past. It's not going to get any easier when people discover that he was a hunter."

"We'll handle the pack." Vadim shrugged. "Besides, it's not like we have to broadcast the fact that Serge was a hunter. All they need to know is that he's your mate."

Niko shook his head. "No, if Serge hopes to be accepted by our pack, then he needs to tell them the truth. They would feel betrayed if they found out later that we didn't tell them. Besides, I think Serge wants to earn their respect in his own way."

"Well, he certainly seems to have won over Ana and Timothy," Vaska said.

Niko swung around to see Serge walking toward him holding hands with both Ana and Timothy. He had a large grin on his face.

"Ana and Timothy have agreed to be part of our family," Serge said. He nodded toward Vadim. "If our alpha approves."

"Is this true?" Vadim asked. "Are you wanting to join Niko, Serge, and Vaska's family?"

Ana and Timothy both nodded.

"You understand that if I allow this, you have to do what they say, right?"

Timothy nodded.

Ana frowned. "Why?" she asked.

"Because they would be in charge of you. It would be their duty to care for you, love you, and teach you to be good wolves."

"If we're bad, are you going to turn us over to the alpha?" Ana asked.

"Ana, I am the alpha."

"No, I mean our old alpha, the one that killed Mommy and Daddy."

"No, Ana, no matter what you decide or how you behave, no one on Vourdala Island will ever turn you over to your old alpha. He was a very bad man, and he should never have been made an alpha."

That answer seemed to satisfy Ana. She nodded her head and stuck her thumb back in her mouth. Niko stared for a moment, waiting for something else to happen, anything else. When Ana just continued to suck on her thumb, Niko turned to look at his brother.

"Satisfied?"

"Are you sure this is what you want to do, all of you?" Vadim asked. "I can tell you from personal experience, children can be a handful. If you think you're going to get any sleep for the next twenty years, you're sadly mistaken."

"There's three of us," Niko said. "I'm sure we can take turns."

"Three of you may not be enough, Niko."

"You and Sasha seem to do okay, and there are only two of you."

"Yeah, but we have a lot of help."

Niko smirked. He knew his brother was weakening. "And we have you."

"Fine." Vadim threw his hands up in the air. "Don't listen to me. Do what you want. Just don't come knocking on my door in the middle of the night when the kids won't sleep."

"So, how do we do this then?" Niko asked.

"You just need to prick their fingers and yours. All of you exchange blood. That should start the bonding process. The rest will come the longer you know each other."

Niko turned to Vaska. "Do you have a needle? I think that would be the least invasive for the children."

Vaska nodded and hurried from the room. Niko turned back to Serge and the two children. Serge looked ready to burst, like he was an expectant father waiting for news of his new child. Niko thought it was cute. It was a side of the strong hunter he hadn't expected.

Niko opened his mouth to say something to Serge about being a big softy when a loud wail on the other side of the room caught his attention. Niko turned to see Markus bringing Juliette into the room, Uri cradled in her arms.

"Vadim, I want you to come meet someone."

Niko led his brother across the room to Markus and Juliette. He smiled at her to reassure her that everything was okay. She clutched

Uri to her chest and looked very nervous. Niko reached out and patted her hand.

"Juliette, Markus, I want you to meet my brother and alpha, Vadim Miroslav. The little man running around like a chicken with its head cut off is Vadim's mate, Sasha." Niko gestured to the trio. "Vadim, this is Markus, Juliette, and Uri."

"So, this is the famous Uri," Vadim said as he held out his hands. "May I?"

Niko nodded when Juliette glanced at him. She handed her son over to Vadim, watching them anxiously. Vadim seemed to be in his element, gently juggling the baby as he crooned down at him.

"He's precious, Juliette. You should be very proud." Vadim nodded to Sasha. "My mate and I have three small ones, two boys and a girl. Our daughter, Riana, is just a few weeks old."

"You have children, alpha?" Juliette asked.

"We do." He chuckled softly. "And let me tell you, once you get to Vourdala Island if you need any help, our housekeeper, Mary, is a godsend. She's helped Sasha and I more times than I can count."

Juliette just nodded. She seemed a little dazed by Vadim.

Vadim handed the baby back then turned toward the crowd in the room. "We need to see if everyone is ready to go. I imagine we only have a few minutes left before the walls get breached. Everyone needs to be ready to go."

"We need help with Antonio," Markus said. "He won't leave his room."

"Antonio?" Vadim asked. "Who's he?"

"It's a long story, Vad," Niko said. "But I don't think it's going to be easy to get him out of his room."

"Let me talk to him," Vaska said.

"We really should just let Vaska get him. Antonio is very…jumpy?" Niko turned and looked at Markus. "Is that a good word?"

"Jumpy, timid, afraid of everything." Markus nodded. "Those all pretty much work."

"If he's going to come with us, he's going to have to deal with me at some point, Niko. You know that."

"I do, Vad, just let Vaska bring him out. Antonio is a special case. He needs...careful handling."

"Then go get Vaska. We need to get out of here while we still can."

Niko nodded and started toward the secret passageway that led to the pantry. He got several steps up the stairs when a large form suddenly blocked his light. Niko cringed back and braced himself for a fight until he recognized Siro, Serge's brother.

"Siro, what are you doing here?" After Serge had his little meltdown and refused to talk to Siro, the man had left.

"You all need to go and go now. The hunters are right behind me."

Niko frowned, all at once noticing that Siro was dressed all in black. "What's going on, Siro? Where's Vaska?"

"I haven't seen him, Niko, and we don't have time to go looking for him."

"I'm not leaving without my mate."

"Niko, we don't have time for this. The hunters are right behind me, and they know exactly where you all are."

"We know. Andrei told them where we were."

Siro frowned. "How did you know that?"

"Andrei believes that Vaska killed his mate. He hates Vaska."

"He's a wolf, too?"

"Yeah." Niko frowned. "Didn't you know that?"

"No, he never said anything and neither did anyone else."

Niko frowned. "Anyone else?" he asked slowly, tensing. He remembered Serge saying something about Siro being a hunter, but he'd passed it off as panic and confusion. Maybe he shouldn't have. "Siro, are you really with the hunters?"

"I am, but not the way you think. I was sent undercover by the Wolf Council to find out what I could. They've heard tidbits of information that makes them think a war is coming between the wolves and the hunters. They want to know if that's true."

"Geez, are you serious?"

Siro nodded and started down the steps. "I am, but I'm also serious about the hunters coming. If you plan to get any of these people out of here before the hunters attack, you all need to go now."

Niko followed Siro back down the steps after the man pushed past him. His heart started pounding faster as adrenaline filled him. "How did you know about the people downstairs?"

"Andrei."

"Right, who else, the shithead," Niko said sarcastically. He balled his hands into fists. "I'd be really interested in getting my hands on that man. He's caused nothing but trouble."

"I might be able to help you with that," Siro replied. "I'm still running with the hunters, one of them so to speak. I can arrange to have Andrei meet you in a dark alley."

"Just how are you running with the hunters? Don't they know you're a wolf?"

"Not so far and I'm hoping to keep it that way. I still have a few things to check out before I report back to the council."

"Like what?" Niko asked a little louder when Siro started moving faster.

"The hunters are planning something, something big. We need to know what it is so that we can plan for it and take precautions. An all-out war between the wolves and the hunters could cause a lot of deaths on both sides."

"Serge might be able to help you with that."

Siro stopped so fast that Niko ran right into him. He grunted and stepped back as Siro turned to look at him.

"Serge is still here?"

Niko frowned. "Yes, didn't you expect him to be?"

"No, not really." Siro shook his head. "He seemed pretty upset when he found out I was his brother."

"He just found out that the people that raised him were probably the ones that killed his family. How did you expect him to behave?"

"Truthfully, I thought he'd leave."

"He's our mate." Niko frowned. "Why would he leave?"

"Because he's spent his entire life being a hunter?"

"He didn't know he was a wolf or a Tri Omega, and he didn't know about me or Vaska."

"You've mated him then?"

Niko nodded.

Siro shook his head. "Good luck to you then."

"You don't sound pleased."

"Oh, I am," Siro said. "Just a little envious. I've been waiting for my mates for a long time. Sometimes it feels like I will never meet them."

Niko stopped suddenly as a thought hit him. "Geez, I keep forgetting that you're twins. That makes you a Tri Omega as well, doesn't it?"

"Yep, same as Serge and our mother."

"You haven't come into your abilities yet, have you?"

Siro frowned. "No, we don't come into our abilities until we find our mates. You know that."

"I do know that, but you wouldn't believe how much I don't know." Niko waved his hand toward the room ahead of them. "Like why Juliette is still alive if her mate died."

"Juliette?"

"She's one of the Tri Omegas down here. Her mate was Vaska's brother Ivan. Vaska had to kill him to save her. She was pregnant and Ivan was trying to kill her. There wasn't anything else he could do."

"Did she accept the mating bite?"

"I assume so."

"If she wasn't bitten, then there shouldn't be a problem. If she was bitten, then as soon as her child is born, she will die."

"Uri was born two days ago."

"Then she wasn't bitten."

"Siro, what happens if one of a mated triad dies?"

"Well, if it's the Tri Omega, then the other two mates will be fine, beyond grieving. They are still bonded to each other and don't need the additive that Tri Omegas need."

"And if Vaska or I were to die?" Niko hated even saying it much less thinking it. The mere idea made the pit of his stomach clench. But he needed to know.

"Tri Omegas are a little different as you well know. Once it's introduced, they need that additive to live. If say, you or Vaska were to die, Serge still needs that additive. The best course of action is to find another mate, preferably a blood relative of the Tri Omega's mate."

"But don't they have just a few days before they start to get sick?"

Siro nodded, and Niko's heart sank. "Yes, but the council is developing a serum that will allow them more time to find a replacement mate. Mind you, the serum won't work long, and it is only supposed to work on Tri Omegas that have fully bonded with their mates, but it will give them a few extra weeks."

"And if they don't find another mate?" Niko held his breath as he waited for Siro to answer. He knew before the man even said anything that he wasn't going to like it. There was too much sadness in Siro's eyes.

"They die."

Chapter 17

Vaska raced into his study and headed for his desk. He knew there had to be a needle in there somewhere. He'd seen one just the other day. He yanked open the first drawer and started searching through. Finding nothing, he went to the second drawer.

A light suddenly snapped on. Vaska jumped and looked up. His blood froze in his veins when he saw Andrei standing by the door, another man he had never seen before standing behind him. Vaska slowly closed the drawer.

"Andrei, I didn't expect to see you here."

"I'm full of surprises," Andrei said, tossing his hands in the air.

"I see you've brought a friend," Vaska replied. "Aren't you going to introduce us?"

Vaska knew that the self-satisfied smirk on Andrei's face didn't bode well for him. Neither did that hate-filled one on the stranger's face as he stepped into the room. The way the man stroked the really big knife in his hand down the side of his face just made him creepy.

"This, my dear Vasiliy, is Boris Venahav. He's in charge of the band of hunters currently scouring your estate."

"What do you want?"

Andrei flicked something off the shoulder of his shirt as he chuckled. "Your head."

"I'm kind of attached to it currently, Andrei, maybe I can get back to you later."

"Ah, now, see, that's the thing." Andrei gestured to Boris. "I've brought Boris along to take care of that problem for you. He's going to separate your head from your body using that nifty little knife he has."

Vaska needed to stall until he could think of some way to escape. He planted his hands on the desk and leaned forward. "Why are you doing this, Andrei? You're just like Ivan. You could have both been happy together with Juliette. Instead you go off half cocked and try and kill her."

"You took Ivan from me!" Andrei snapped, his face suddenly turning red.

"No, Ivan did that. He tried to kill Juliette. I couldn't allow him to do that."

"She deserved to die. She tried to take Ivan from me."

"Andrei, you really are an idiot. Juliette was Ivan's mate."

"Ivan was my mate!"

"True, he was, but he was also Juliette's mate." Vaska knew he might die in the next few minutes, but at least he would have the satisfaction of watching the truth start to dawn on Andrei. "She was also your mate, Andrei. Juliette was a Tri Omega."

"You're lying!" Andrei shouted. He suddenly started rapidly pacing back and forth across the floor. "I would have known if she was my mate."

"Ivan knew."

"I don't believe you."

"So, don't believe me." Vaska shrugged. "That doesn't make it any less true."

"NO!" Andrei screamed. Boris looked startled by Andrei's sudden outburst. He started backing away as Andrei fell to his knees.

"Guess you didn't expect that, did you, Andrei? Your *mate* tried to kill your other mate. You tried to kill her. You might have had an excuse because you thought Juliette was trying to take Ivan from you, but he had no excuse. He got Juliette pregnant and when he found out, he tried to kill her."

"Juliette's still alive?" Andrei asked as he jumped to his feet and ran over to the desk. "Where is she?"

"What does it matter, Andrei?" Vaska gestured to the hunter standing in the doorway watching them both cautiously. "You've brought in the hunters. I doubt Juliette or her child will live through the night."

"Her child?" Andrei whispered. "Ivan's child?"

"Yes."

The hunter must have seen Andrei tense and start to shift, because he took off running. Andrei shifted and took off after him. Vaska took a second to draw in a deep breath then ran from the room. He wasn't planning on going after Andrei. His destination was the basement and the people depending on him.

He could hear fighting and the sounds of stuff crashing to the floor as he ran past the dining room and into the kitchen. A quick glance showed Andrei and the hunter fighting, both with blood dripping from them. Vaska couldn't tell which one was winning, and he didn't have time to stop and ask.

Vaska smelled something different the moment he stepped into the kitchen. The lights were also out. Vaska let his lupine eyes take over and extended his claws then lifted his nose into the air, taking a deep sniff of air.

The first thing he noticed was that Siro had recently been through the kitchen. He'd recognize the man's scent anywhere. It was close to Serge's unique smell but didn't hold the same attraction for Vaska.

The second thing that Vaska noticed was that someone else was in the room with him. He couldn't quite figure out where he was because his scent was muted, but Vaska knew he was there somewhere.

Most emotions gave off a scent of some sort, one that wolves could smell. Hate gave off a putrid scent, almost acidic. If the hate was strong enough, it could actually make someone's eyes water. This hate was very strong.

There was an underlying scent of fear though. Whoever was in the room knew Vaska was there, and he was afraid. Vaska used that to his advantage. He scraped his claws along the countertop as he turned in a complete circle. The sound they made was deafening in the silence.

"I know you're there," Vaska said slowly. "I can smell you."

Nothing, not a peep. This hunter was smart. Vaska started walking around the island in the middle of the kitchen, and it was a big kitchen. It took more than a few steps. He couldn't see anything that looked out of place, but he didn't spend that much time in the kitchen. This was Markus's domain.

"Are you going to come out and face me like a man or hide like the coward you are?"

"Why should I?" a voice said from across the room.

Vaska instantly turned in that direction and tried to figure out exactly where the voice came from. He tensed when he didn't see anything except the large fridge and shelves of dishes.

"You're not a man."

Vaska jerked around when the voice suddenly sounded like it came from behind him. His heart started to pound a little faster. Whoever this hunter was, he was playing with Vaska, and he was enjoying it.

"Are you afraid to face me?" Vaska asked.

"Do I seem stupid to you?" The man chuckled. "You're a wolf. You could slice me in half without breaking a sweat."

Vaska spun around when the voice sounded from the other side of the room. He didn't know how this man was moving so quietly, but he had sneaking down to an art form. Vaska hadn't even heard him move. And that worried him.

"Then why come here?"

"To kill you, Ivan."

Vaska blinked, suddenly confused. "I'm not Ivan."

"Do you really expect me to believe that?"

"It's the truth."

"You lie!" The words were hissed into Vaska's ear.

Vaska swallowed hard when he felt a sharp blade move across his throat. It wasn't deep enough to kill him or even draw blood, but just enough to let Vaska know it was there and to not struggle.

"My name is Vasiliy Federov. I killed my brother Ivan six months ago."

"Prove it."

"How? He's dead and buried."

"Then I guess I'll just have to take your head then."

Vaska felt the blade start to sink into his throat. He closed his eyes for a split second and sent up a prayer that his mates might make it out alive along with the other Tri Omegas. Opening his eyes, Vaska went into action.

He drove his arm up between his body and the arm of the man trying to kill him. At the same moment, he shoved his elbow back into the man's gut. Vaska had the satisfaction of hearing the man grunt, but it was short lived. He could feel the blade cut across his skin and then the sudden cold feeling of blood dripping down his neck.

Vaska didn't know how injured he was, but he could still swallow, so that had to mean something. As the man tried to cut at him again, Vaska grabbed his arm and pulled as hard as he could.

Much to Vaska's surprise, the man went flying over his shoulder, landing on the floor in front of him in a heap. Before Vaska could blink, the man arched his body and hopped up, landing on both feet. He swung around to sneer at Vaska, his knife held high in the air.

"It's not going to be that easy, Ivan."

"I'm not Ivan."

"I don't believe you."

The grin on the man's face seemed out of place, malicious almost. It sent a spike of cold hard fear spiraling down Vaska's spine. This man really did plan to kill him. He didn't seem to care that Vaska wasn't Ivan.

"I'm telling you, I'm not Ivan. I killed him six months ago when he tried to kill his mate, Juliette."

"Juliette?" The man froze for a moment then the knife in his hand started slowly lowering. "Juliette is still alive?"

Vaska didn't really know how to answer that question. It seemed to be very important to the hunter, but Vaska could find no good reason to give the man any information that might lead him to Juliette or the others.

"I can't tell you that."

The knife went up in the air again. "Because you don't know or because she's already dead."

"Because I refuse to give you any information that could lead to her death. You can kill me first."

The man blinked. "You really aren't Ivan, are you?"

"No."

"You're his brother?"

Vaska raised his hands in a friendly gesture. "Look, I don't know what your interest is in Juliette, but—"

"Juliette is my sister. I've been looking for her for months."

"You're not a hunter?"

"No."

"Prove it."

The man smirked and set the knife down on the kitchen island. A moment later he flicked out his claws and waved them in front of Vaska. "Happy?"

"Not yet." Vaska held up a finger and called to his mates. *"Niko, Serge, I need one of you to ask Juliette what her brother's name is."*

"You need what?" Niko answered back.

"I need to know the name of Juliette's brother."

"Now?"

"Niko, I'm in the kitchen with a man that swears he's Juliette's brother. If he and I can't come to an agreement, he's probably going to try and kill me. I just need some answers."

"I'm on my way," Serge said.

"Just be careful. This guy is really jumpy."

"Juliette says her brother's name is Robert."

Vaska lowered his hand and looked at the man. "What is your name?"

"Robert."

"Now it's your turn. How do I know you're telling the truth?"

"I assume you're talking to someone?"

"I am."

"Your mate?"

Singular mate. Vaska wasn't about to inform the man that he had two mates instead of one. "Yes."

"When Juliette was a baby, she couldn't pronounce my name. She couldn't even say Robby. She used to call me Ribby."

"This man says she called him Ribby," Vaska said to Niko through their bond. *"Check with Juliette and ask her if that's true. Also ask if there is any other way to identify him."*

"Okay, give me a moment."

Vaska watched the man's eyebrow arch as the seconds ticked by. The waiting was excruciating. Vaska expected the man to go for the knife at any moment. He was a little shocked when he didn't, just standing there in silence instead.

"You know coming here like this wasn't your best choice, right?" Vaska asked.

"Is killing someone ever a good choice?" the man asked.

"We're under siege here. Hunters are roaming the property as we speak."

"I know. I came with them."

Vaska paused for a moment then stepped back. "You came with the hunters?"

"I did."

"Can you think of a single reason I shouldn't let my mate kill you where you stand?"

"Your mate?" the man chuckled.

Vaska pointed to the man standing in the doorway to the pantry, the man he had just spotted. "Him."

The man swung around. His hand started to inch toward the knife on the counter. Vaska quickly reached out and pressed one of his claws against the man's jugular vein. "Make a move toward him and it will be your last."

"I thought your mate was checking on things for you?"

"My mate is, my other mate." Vaska smirked as he looked across the room at Serge. "I'm lucky enough to have two mates."

"Does that…does that mean Juliette is still alive?"

"She is, and she's under my protection."

"I just want to see her." Vaska felt the man's throat move against his hand as he swallowed. "I won't hurt her, I swear."

"You came with the hunters. That right there means I don't believe you."

"I had to come with the hunters. It was the only way I could find you, find Juliette."

"And yet you want me to let you know where she is?" Vaska laughed harshly. "I wouldn't be a very good protector if I just let you have that information, now would I?"

"Please, tie me up, gag me, do whatever you need to do. I just want to see my sister."

"Why should I?"

"She was taken from me."

"By Ivan?" Vaska really had no idea how Juliette and Ivan met. He had been away at school when it happened. He was surprised when the man shook his head.

"Not exactly. Yes, Ivan was involved, but my parents basically sold Juliette to him. My father is the alpha of our pack. When they met for business, Ivan met Juliette. He seemed to know that they were mates. He convinced my father to sell Juliette to him. She was gone before I could stop it."

"Your father and alpha sold your sister?"

"Yes." At least the man didn't sound happy about that fact.

"Didn't he know what she was?"

"I knew, and our mother knew. We never told Father. Our mother was too afraid that Juliette would be taken away by the council, so she made us swear to secrecy."

"Vaska, Juliette says her brother was called Ribby," Niko broke in. *"She also says that he has a crescent shaped scare on his left wrist from when she bit him as a toddler."*

"Let me see your left wrist," Vaska said to the man.

The man held up his wrist. Vaska pulled the cuff of his shirt down until he saw a small crescent-shaped scar. Vaska tapped it with his finger. "How did you get this?"

"Juliette bit me when I wouldn't share my toys with her. She was five."

"Niko," Vaska said to his mate as he let go of the man's wrist, *"it looks like we might have Juliette's brother up here. Does she want to see him?"*

There was a moment of silence then Niko replied. *"She says she will see him, but she will not go home with him."*

"Okay, we're coming down, Niko."

"Be careful."

"Come on let's go," Vaska said as he pushed the guy in front of him toward the pantry and Serge. "You're sister wants to see you, but only as long as you understand that she will not be going home with you. Her place is with us now."

"I understand, and I wouldn't take her home even if she wanted to go there. Our father would just sell her again to the highest bidder."

"You're father sounds like a great guy," Serge said as Vaska and Robby reached him.

"Oh yeah, he's a real peach," Robby replied.

Serge chuckled as he walked into the pantry. Vaska rolled his eyes and pushed Robby in after his mate. He started to step inside when a sudden noise behind him made him swing around, crouching down with his claws drawn.

He looked across the room and saw Andrei stumbling into the room. Vaska inhaled sharply when Andrei stepped into a bit of light shining in through the window from the moon outside. He was covered in blood, dragging his leg behind him. Andrei was a mess.

"Andrei?" Vaska whispered as he stood up.

"I killed him, Vasiliy," Andrei gasped. "I killed Boris and the others. They can't hurt Juliette or the baby anymore."

Vaska blinked as Andrei fell to the floor. Once his shock wore off, he ran over and knelt on the floor next to the man. He looked for a place to touch Andrei that wouldn't hurt him, but he couldn't find one. Every inch of Andrei's body looked damaged. Vaska finally settled on holding Andrei's hand.

"I did it, Vasiliy."

"You killed them all?"

"I missed one, but he wasn't a hunter. He's one of us."

"I think he's talking about Siro, Vaska," Serge said from behind them. "He's downstairs with Niko."

Vaska winced when Andrei coughed and blood dribbled out of his mouth. "Andrei, you're in pretty bad shape."

"I'm dying, and I know it."

Vaska couldn't argue with the man. He was dying.

"Let me see Juliette and the baby, please?" Andrei's words beseeched Vaska. "Just once before I die. I need to see them, see Ivan's child."

"Andrei—"

"Please, Vasiliy." Andrei's bloody fingers clutched at Vaska's shirt.

"Niko, can you bring Juliette and Uri upstairs?"

"What?"

"Please, just do as I ask."

"What about the hunters?"

"I think they are all dead."

"Seriously?"

"I think so. Maybe you should bring Siro up as well. He can start searching the house to see if we have any intruders left."

"Yeah, okay. I'll leave Vadim and Sasha down her to look after everyone else."

"Good idea." Great idea, actually. Vaska was so wrapped up in everything that was happening, he had momentarily forgotten about everyone else.

"Niko is bringing Juliette and the baby upstairs, Andrei."

"Tell…tell Niko I'm sorry I tried to kill him."

"You can tell him yourself when he gets up here."

Andrei's hand smacked against Vaska's chest a couple of times. "I'm sorry for all the trouble I caused, Vasiliy. I just…I thought—"

"It's okay, Andrei. I know what you thought."

"It's not okay." Andrei yanked on Vaska's shirt. "It's not okay. I—"

Andrei suddenly started coughing again. By the time he was done, Vaska could hear Niko, Siro, and Juliette coming into the room. He glanced over his shoulder and gestured for Juliette to come closer.

"Come here, Juliette."

Juliette looked hesitant but then started across the room, pausing when she passed her brother. She gave him a long look then hurried past him. When she reached Vaska's side and saw Andrei lying on the floor, she cringed.

"No, no, it's okay. He's not going to hurt you, Juliette. He's dying. He just wants to see you and the baby."

"Dying?" Juliette whispered as she looked down at Andrei.

"He killed the hunters to save you and Uri."

Juliette frowned. "Why?"

"Andrei thought you were trying to take Ivan away from him, that you were trying to steal his mate," Vaska explained. "He didn't understand that you were all mates, Juliette, not until it was too late."

"Didn't he understand that it was supposed to be the three of us together?"

"No, he—"

"I'm sorry, Juliette," Andrei whispered. "I didn't know there were three of us. I thought Ivan was *my* mate, not ours. He never told me. He just said I was his mate. He said you were just a passing fling."

Vaska heard Juliette gasp and felt sorry for her. His brother Ivan was more than a killer, he was a bastard. He had the world in the palm of his hands, and he lost it by playing games with his mates.

Vaska glanced over his shoulder to where Niko and Serge stood and swore to himself he would do everything in his power to insure both his mates knew how much he wanted them. He wasn't going to lose them by playing games.

"Can I..." Andrei called out, drawing Vaska's attention. He watched the man lick his lips. "Can I see him?"

Vaska reached out and helped Juliette sit down on the floor next to Andrei. She still wasn't moving too fast. Juliette uncovered the baby's face and lowered him down so that Andrei could see him.

"Oh," Andrei murmured. "He's beautiful, Juliette."

"He looks like Ivan, don't you think?" Juliette asked.

Vaska was amazed that she could even speak Ivan's name let alone say that her baby looked like him. Ivan was a monster, and they both knew it. Still, with the way Juliette was looking at Andrei and the tears gathering in her eyes, she must have known Andrei was dying.

"He does," Andrei said. "But I think he looks like you, too. Hopefully, you'll have more influence on him than Ivan or me. You can teach him to be a good man, not like us."

"You're not a bad man, Andrei," Juliette replied. "Ivan lied to you."

"I'm not a good man, Juliette. But maybe...maybe you won't tell him that, huh? Maybe you can tell him I would have been a good man for him."

Vaska felt tears prickle the corners of his eyes as he watched Juliette reach down and brush the hair back from Andrei's bruised face.

"I'll tell him that you saved us both."

"I'd like that."

Andrei suddenly started coughing again. Vaska helped Juliette grab the baby and move back. When Andrei quieted down, he was wheezing, Vaska knew the man didn't have long in this world. When Juliette held Uri out to him, Vaska took him and cradled the baby to his chest.

He could barely stand it when Juliette leaned down close to Andrei and smoothed more hair back from his face before leaning down to place a gentle kiss on Andrei's lips. Tears were falling from her eyes when she leaned back.

"I'll tell him all about you, Andrei, I promise," Juliette whispered through her tears. "I'll tell him how much you loved his father and how you died trying to save us. Uri will be proud of you. I'll make sure of it."

"I don't deserve it," Andrei murmured.

Vaska could see the light starting to fade from Andrei's eyes and could barely choke back his protest. Andrei wasn't a good man, he was right about that. But in Vaska's eyes, he had redeemed himself by saving them all.

"You let me worry about what you deserve, Andrei," Juliette said. "You just rest."

Andrei nodded and closed his eyes, a small smile moving across his lips. A moment later, Uri started crying. Vaska looked down and saw that Andrei wasn't breathing anymore. Juliette leaned down and brushed her lips over Andrei's one more time then sat back and reached for Uri.

She looked up at Vaska, tears streaming down her face. "Can we go home now?"

Chapter 18

"Mary, have you seen Ana?" Serge asked as he walked into the kitchen. "It's her bath time, and she's disappeared."

Mary laughed and pointed toward the dining room. "Check under the table. That's the last place I saw her."

Serge rolled his eyes and walked toward the dining room. Ana was turning out to be quite the handful. She was a delightful girl with a sharp mind, sometimes too sharp. She seemed to run circles around everyone that met her. All she had to do was bat her eyelashes and suck her thumb and people melted at her feet.

Still, Serge wouldn't trade a single day of the last three weeks with Ana and Timothy in his life for anything. Being a brand new parent to two children wasn't easy, but it had its rewards. Chasing Ana down for bath time wasn't one of them.

Serge walked into the dining room and eyed the table. It was a large one, big enough to sit everyone that lived in the alpha compound and then some. Ana was four years old. She could easily hide under it.

Serge walked over to table and flipped up the white table cloth and peered under it. No Ana. He dropped the tablecloth and glanced around the room. He couldn't see another place that she could hide, but there was another door.

Serge sighed and walked toward the door. Just as he reached it, the door swung open and Siro walked in, Robby right behind him.

"Serge, just the man I was looking for," Siro said.

"Oh?"

"Robby and I need to head out. We have to report to the council and then get back to the hunter compound. I told the hunters we were following a lead on the great Vasiliy Federov, but that will only hold them for so long. If we don't get back, they are going to start to suspect something."

"Geez, Siro, did you have to use Vaska's name?"

Siro shrugged. "He's pretty high up on the list, and once I tell them that he was killed while fighting Andrei, I hope to get him off that list all together and off their radar."

Serge frowned even as relief flooded him. "Do you think they will believe you?"

Siro gestured to the man standing behind him. "Robby has dried blood on his knife from when he attacked Vasiliy in the kitchen three weeks ago. Once the hunters test it, they'll believe me. I just don't think it's a good idea for Vasiliy to leave the island anytime soon, you know what I mean?"

Serge nodded, grateful that his brother was willing to go to such measure to keep his mate safe. "What about Niko?"

"I'm afraid I have nothing on him right now. He seems to have disappeared from that Russian village he was staying in. A bunch of his stuff was still in his room." Siro shrugged. "My guess is that another wolf killed him."

Serge chuckled. "Thanks."

Siro reached out and slapped Serge on the shoulder. "Anytime, but I expect the same when I find my mates."

"When you find your other mate, you mean." Serge shook his finger at Siro. "You've already found one of them, and you know it."

Siro shook his head, looking grim. "Maybe, but I can't claim him, not right now. It's too dangerous."

"Siro, if what we suspect is true and the hunters are mounting a war against us, the danger won't go away any time soon. Don't give up what you can have with your mates because you're scared."

"I'm not scared, Serge, I just—"

"You're terrified," Serge snorted. "Stop lying to yourself."

Siro rolled his eyes.

"You know I'm telling you the truth, Siro. I almost lost Vaska and Niko. I know what I'm talking about."

"And do you think that a few days with them is worth putting their lives in danger?"

"I believe that every second we have together is worth it, Siro. Together, we are stronger than we are apart."

"I'll think about it."

"You do that."

Serge had no doubt that his brother would think about it. He couldn't help but do it. Now that he had found one of his mates, even if he hadn't mated the man, Siro wouldn't be able to think of much else. It kind of worked that way.

"How's your sister, Robby?" Serge asked, purposely turning the conversation away from Siro when he saw his brother frown. Siro would have to make up his own mind.

"She seems to be doing okay. She likes working in the bakery. Pauline lets her bring Uri with her to work."

"How's she coping?"

Robby shrugged. "She says she's okay, but I think she missed what could have been if Ivan and Andrei had claimed her. Legend says that if she lost her mates there are others out there for her, that fate wouldn't let her live her life without them, but I don't know. It just kind of seems like a platitude that they tell people when they lose their mates. I don't know how much of it is real and how much is myth."

"Well, myth or no myth," Serge said, "let's hope that she finds new mates and that they are better for her than Ivan and Andrei."

"Yeah."

"Serge," Siro said, "I wish you'd reconsider and come back to the council headquarters to meet Remus."

Serge pushed his hands into the pocket of his jeans and glanced down at his feet. "I will at some point. I'm just not ready yet."

"He's our father, Serge. He hasn't seen you since you were five years old, not since the day our mother and other father died. He wants to see you."

"I will."

"Serge, he thought you were dead all of this time. Don't punish him for not looking for you."

"I'm not, I just—how could he think I was dead?" Serge asked. "There was no body, no nothing. He found you alive. Why couldn't he find me, too?"

"Because the hunters took you. You know that. He found me because the hunters thought I was dead and left me behind."

Serge shook his head. "He should have kept looking for me. I would have."

"Damn it, Serge, he had just lost his mates, both of them. I was injured and in a coma. He couldn't find you and assumed you had been killed too. It's not unheard of for the hunters to take a body back to their compound as evidence that they had gotten a kill. A five-year-old child is easier to carry than a full-grown adult."

"Look." Serge reached up and rubbed his hand over the back of his neck. "I'm not going to get into this with you right now. I need to find Ana and get her into her bath. It's almost her bedtime, and I have plans with my mates after the kids are in bed."

"This is wrong, Serge. You know it is."

"And maybe we'll discuss it with you when you come back to visit. Right now, I'm going to go find Ana."

Siro rolled his eyes. "Fine, we'll discuss it when I get back, but I'm not going to let this drop, Serge. Our father has a right to see you. If you change your mind, he's at the council headquarters. You can contact him directly or have someone get a message to me."

"Aren't you headed right back to the hunters?"

"I will be as soon as I report to the council. They're sending me right back out on another mission." Serge waved his hand absently in the air before crossing his arms over his chest. "Something about people being added to the hunter's hit list."

"You'll be careful, right?"

"I'm always careful, Serge. It's the only way I've stayed alive all these years."

"Well, I don't have to like it. You put your ass in the line of fire way too often. The council needs to give you break, or at least our father should."

"And he would if he could tell the council who I really was. You need to remember that the Wolf Council doesn't know that we are Remus's children. He had to keep us secret so that they wouldn't take us from our parents. If word gets out that we're his sons, a lot of shit will hit the fan."

Serge frowned. "Do you think there's ever going to come a time when Tri Omegas aren't treated like commodities to be bartered and traded around?"

"I certainly hope so." Siro gestured to the room around them. "Vadim providing sanctuary here on Vourdala Island to any Tri Omega who wants it is a step in the right direction. I imagine you'll have a whole lot more coming in the dark days ahead."

Serge nodded. He knew Siro was right. The closer the wolves and hunters came to war, the more Tri Omegas would be hunted by both for their abilities—the wolves to harness the powers of the Tri Omegas and the hunters to kill them before they could mate and develop their powers. Life wasn't going to be easy for anyone if war couldn't be averted.

"Vadim has already put plans into action to keep everyone safe here on the island. He's cut off the tourist stuff except for special occasions and holidays and then only after everyone has been screened. He's also started patrols throughout the island."

"Yeah, I saw them earlier. He's creating his own little army."

"Can you blame the man?" Serge asked. "His entire island is filling up with Tri Omegas. We've already had requests for four more to come to the Island and that doesn't even include the alphas that have been threatening to land on his beaches so they can get their own Tri Omega. They seem to think Vadim is gathering his own army of Tri Omegas and not sharing with anyone else."

"He can handle it." Siro smirked. "Vadim has always struck me as a man who works well under pressure."

"Have you met Sasha?" Serge snickered as he thought about the crazy little man. "Vadim has to be cool under pressure otherwise he'd strangle his mate in a week. That man's certifiable."

"But he does adore Vadim."

"He does." Serge smiled. "I've never seen a man so crazy about his mate."

"Have you looked in the mirror lately?"

Serge felt his face flush, but he couldn't deny Siro's words. He did adore his mates. The last three weeks being mated to Vaska and Niko had been some of the best days of his life. He didn't regret a single one of them, and he hoped for many more.

"Yeah, well."

Siro chuckled. "Okay, Robby and I are going to take off. Take care of those two mates of yours, and my new niece and nephew. I should be back this way in a few weeks."

Serge nodded then decided to toss his brother a bone since he was going into a dangerous situation and might not be coming back. "We'll talk more about Remus when you come back, okay?"

"I'd like that." Siro smiled. "I'd like that a lot."

"Be safe, bro."

"Always."

Serge didn't know how he felt as Siro and Robby walked out of the dining room. He had spent a lot of time with Siro over the last three weeks, but he still felt like he barely knew the man. Siro seemed to like being mysterious.

Still, having Siro back in his life filled a hole in Serge's heart that he didn't know was there, even if he was still trying to get used to calling his brother Siro instead of Yurok. He just wished Siro would let up on going to meet his father.

He wasn't ready, and he didn't know when he would be. The thought of meeting Remus made Serge's stomach turn every time he thought about it, and Serge didn't know why. He thought he would have been overjoyed that his father was still alive. He was just scared.

Maybe it had to do with what happened when he was a child. Maybe it had to do with growing up with the hunters. Or maybe it had to do with the fact that he was just scared of meeting his father after all of these years. Whatever it was, Serge wanted to put it off as long as he could.

Serge cocked his head to one side when he heard a spike of laughter in the hallway. He'd recognize that soft little laugh anywhere. He'd heard it more and more over the last three weeks as Ana became used to being loved and safe.

Serge chuckled and pushed open the dining room door that led into the hallway. He was a little surprised to see Vadim starting up the stairs, Ana tossed over his shoulder. The big alpha still made him a little uneasy.

"Vadim?"

Vadim turned, a bright smile on his face. "Oh hey, has Niko found you yet?"

"No, why?"

"He's looking for you. He asked Sasha and me to take the kids for a few hours." Vadim grinned. "He said something about him and Vaska fulfilling a hunter's desires?"

Serge's interest was instantly peaked. "Oh? And just where would my wayward mates be?"

Vadim smirked. "You're the hunter. You find them."

Serge gaped as he watched Vadim turn and walk up the stairs, Ana laughing and waving from her position over the man's shoulder. Serge lifted his hand and waved back then blew Ana a kiss before turning away.

So, his mates had something special planned and he was supposed to hunt them down, huh? Serge stuck his nose in the air and drew in a deep breath. He caught the faint whiff of coffee brewing somewhere. He assumed in the kitchen.

He could also smell the fragrance of trees and fresh air blowing in from outside. It was overlaid with a scent of his mates. A small smile coming over his lips, Serge started toward the front door and the great outdoors. He suspected his mates were waiting for him outside.

The closer to the door he got, the stronger the scent became. Stepping out into the small courtyard of the alpha compound, Serge was suddenly overwhelmed with the strong masculine scent of his mates.

Serge groaned as his cock instantly reacted and hardened. He wasn't surprised though. Even after three weeks it seemed all he had to do was smell his mates or see them and he was hard as a rock. Vaska and Niko aroused him more than anyone he ever met.

"I know you're out here," Serge said through their bond. *"I can smell you."*

"What else can you smell, majiktoka?" Vaska asked.

Serge sniffed the air again then inhaled sharply as the sweet scent of his mates' arousal filled his senses. He didn't know exactly where they were or what they were doing, but he knew they were fooling around.

Serge sniffed in every direction until one became stronger than the other. He started in that direction, following the scent until the sounds of sex overcame the scent. Serge's heart started pounding when he heard Niko moaning, the sound of flesh slapping against flesh filling the forest around him.

He ripped his shirt off as he started hurrying through the trees in the direction of Niko's soft cries. By the time he broke through the trees, Serge stood naked, his clothes dropped carelessly on the ground behind him.

He pressed his hand over his rapidly beating heart as he took in the scene before him. A large blanket had been spread out over the ground. A picnic basket sat several feet away. The entire area was lit up with a series of torches set in the ground in a wide circle around the blanket.

Smack dab in the middle of the torches were Vaska and Niko. Vaska had Niko on his knees as he plunged into his ass from behind. Niko was pushing back against Vaska, moaning and groaning with every thrust.

Serge groaned and grabbed his cock, stroking it as quickly as he could. He was so aroused he thought he might combust just from watching his two mates fuck each other. He didn't think he'd ever seen anything so magnificent in his life.

Niko glanced over at him and winked. "I got something better for you than that hand. Vaska's already slicked up and waiting for you."

Serge's eyes bugged out of his head. He couldn't move across the space separating him from his mates fast enough. There had been a lot of sex between the three of them over the last three weeks, but somehow, Serge had always missed out on fucking Vaska. It just kind of turned out that way.

He dropped to his knees behind Vaska and pressed his fingers between the man's ass cheeks. He groaned when his fingers instantly slid right into Vaska's ass. Arousal beat like a drum inside his head.

Serge could barely function. He couldn't think of anything but how good it was going to feel to sink his aching cock inside Vaska's tight ass. It was the one thought in his head, overriding everything else.

He pulled his fingers out and lined the head of his cock up with Vaska's tight hole, waiting for the next time Vaska pulled back from Niko. The moment Vaska pulled back, Serge pushed in.

His groan of satisfaction filled the area as Vaska's body took him right in to the root. When the rhythm of Vaska's thrust made the man pull away, Serge almost cried out in protest, but before he could, Vaska was back, enveloping his cock once again.

"Fuck!"

"Yes, fuck, Serge," Niko cried out. "Fuck him faster, harder."

Serge gripped Vaska's hips and did as Niko demanded. He pounded into Vaska as hard and as fast as he could. Each thrust was met with Vaska's body pushing back against his. The man's tight, silken muscles gripped Serge's cock until he thought his body might explode.

"Oh yes, Serge, he likes that," Niko called out. "He really likes that. I can feel it every time you thrust into him. His cock thickens. Serge, it's throbbing inside of me."

"Yeah?" he leaned over and growled into Vaska's ear. Niko's words were driving Serge out of his mind. "Do you like my cock in your ass, Vaska?"

Vaska nodded rapidly, his breath coming out in heavy pants. Serge could feel the man's inner muscles starting to repeatedly clamp down on his cock with such force that Serge had a hard time moving in and out of Vaska's ass.

"I like fucking you, Vaska. I like filling you while you squeeze my cock. Gonna do this every day for the rest of our lives. Gonna fuck you and Niko every day, mate."

"Yes!" Vaska shouted as his body suddenly went stiff, and his head fell back to rest against Serge's shoulder.

Serge couldn't stand it. His cock was being held in a vice grip and massaged with each throb of Vaska's body as the man emptied himself into Niko's ass. Niko was crying out beneath Vaska in such a way that Serge could only assume the man was coming.

Serge gripped Vaska's hips harder and thrust into his ass as far as he could go. At the same time, he leaned down and sank his teeth into the curve of Vaska's neck. The sweet-tasting essence of his mate filled his mouth at the same time he filled Vaska's ass with his release.

Serge growled loudly and humped his hips a couple of more times. His cock throbbed and pulsed and gave up so much seed Serge wondered if he'd ever be able to come again. He extracted his teeth from Vaska's neck and licked the bite mark clean then planted several kisses along the line of his jaw.

"Thank you, baby," he whispered through their bond.

"For what?" Vaska asked as he arched his neck to give Serge better access.

"For everything," Serge replied. *"For Niko, for saving me and mating me, for giving me this life."*

"My pleasure, mate."

Serge chuckled and humped his hips again, chuckling when he heard both Niko and Vaska groan at his movements. *"No, I'm pretty sure this was my pleasure."*

"It was our pleasure, Serge," Niko said.

"Don't fool yourself, Niko," Serge said out loud. "I hunted you both down and found exactly what I didn't know I wanted. It was definitely my pleasure."

THE END

WWW.STORMYGLENN.COM

ABOUT THE AUTHOR

Stormy believes the only thing sexier than a man in cowboy boots is two or three men in cowboy boots. She also believes in love at first sight, soul Mates, true love, and happy endings.

Stormy lives in the great Northwest region of the USA, with her gorgeous husband and soul Mate, six very active teenagers, two boxer/collie puppies, one old biddy cat, and one fish.

You can usually find her cuddled in bed with a book in her hand and a puppy in her lap, or on her laptop, creating the next sexy man for one of her stories. Stormy welcomes comments from readers. You can find her website at www.stormyglenn.com

Also by Stormy Glenn

Blaecleah Brothers 1: *Cowboy Easy*
Blaecleah Brothers 2: *Cowboy Keeper*
Wolf Creek Pack 1: *Full Moon Mating*
Wolf Creek Pack 2: *Just A Taste Of Me*
Wolf Creek Pack 3: *Tasty Treats: Volume 3, Man to Man*
Wolf Creek Pack 4: *Blood Prince*
Wolf Creek Pack 5: *Love, Always, Promise*
Wolf Creek Pack 6: *Who's Afraid of the Big Bad Wolf?*
Wolf Creek Pack 7: *Pretty Baby*
Tri-Omega Mates 1: *Secret Desires*
Tri-Omega Mates 2: *Forbidden Desires*
Tri-Omega Mates 3: *Hidden Desires*
Tri-Omega Mates 4: *Stolen Desires*
Tri-Omega Mates 5: *Unspoken Desires*
Lovers of Alpha Squad 1: *Mari's Men*
Lovers of Alpha Squad 2: *The Doctor's Patience*
Lovers of Alpha Squad 3: *Julia's Knight*
Lovers of Alpha Squad 4: *Three of a Kind*
Love's Legacy 1: *Cowboy Legacy*
Love's Legacy 2: *Cowboy Dreams*
Sweet Perfection 1: *Sweet Treats*
Sweet Perfection 2: *Mr. Wonderful*
True Blood Mate 1: *Heart Song*
True Blood Mate 2: *Alpha Born*
True Blood Mate 3: *Love Sexy*
Katzman 1: *The Katzman's Mate*
Katzman 2: *Dream Mate*
Katzman 3: *Pride Mate*
My Lupine Lover
The Master's Pet
Wolf Queen
His Gentle Touch
Fire Demon
Mating Heat

Also by Stormy Glenn and Joyee Flynn

Delta Wolf 1: *Chameleon Wolf*
Delta Wolf 2: *Mating Games*
Delta Wolf 3: *Blood Lust*

Available at
BOOKSTRAND.COM

Siren Publishing, Inc.
www.SirenPublishing.com

9 781610 345019